PRAISE FOR ANDREA RANDALL

November Blue

The women in this series are bold, strong and independent. Yet they aren't intimidating or stone cold. Their hearts are vulnerable, they are loyal with a passion, and they love deeply and intensely. ~ **Flirty and Dirty Book Blog**

The heated scenes between Bo and Ember were magic. ~ **Tough Critic Book Reviews**

Andrea Randall has a way with words and I can't wait to see what emotion she stirs up next ~ **Candy Coated Book Blog**

Who ever said that the sequel never lives up to the original never read an Andrea Randall book! ~ **The Book Avenue**

I love that this is no cookie cutter romance and it felt more like poetry...or a song than a book at times. ~ **Michelle Pace, co-author of The Sound Wave Series**

It's hard not to get sucked into the world of Ember and Bo ~ **SMI Book Club**

...an excellent writer with a superb talent at crafting words ... that grab ahold of your heart ... An eloquent, master wordsmith - **All the Raeje Book Blog**

I could gush about this book for days...If you read one book of Andrea Randall's this should be it. There's something in here for EVERYONE to love. ~ **Word Blog**

In the Stillness

They had the kind of love that just makes you shake. Cry. Laugh. Ache right down to your soul. It was an irreplaceable love. The kind that, once taken away leaves a hole that no other person can ever fill. ~**Aestas Book Blog**

Gorgeous writing. Eloquent, but in a raw, realistic way. A delicate subject matter, distressing thoughts, and yet, a wondrous growth that the reader experiences every step of the way, with the characters. ~**Maryse's Book Blog**

This is easily the best book I've read all year, and I will be hard-pressed to find a book that will bring out of me such a strong reaction as this book. In the Stillness is a stimulant of the best and worst kind; it is truly captivating and commensurate with the suffering of so many in society. ~ **Romantic Reading Escapes Book Blog**

Author Andrea Randall has written a gut-wrenching, 5++ star piece of dark perfection. This is a journey of redemption, healing, loving, acceptance, and moving forward. ~ **K and T Book Reviews**

MARRYING EMBER

A NOVEMBER BLUE

NOVELLA

ANDREA RANDALL

BOOKS BY ANDREA RANDALL

November Blue

Ten Days of Perfect
Reckless Abandon
Sweet Forty-Two
Marrying Ember
Bo & Ember

In The Stillness
Nocturne (with Charles Sheehan-Miles)
Something's Come Up (with Michelle Pace)

MARRYING
EMBER

IF YOU ENJOYED THIS BOOK, PLEASE SHARE IT WITH A FRIEND, WRITE A REVIEW ONLINE, OR SEND FEEDBACK TO THE AUTHORS!

www.andrearandall.com

Copyright © 2014 Andrea Randall.

All rights reserved. No part of this publication may be reproduced, distributed, or transmitted in any form or by any means, including photocopying, recording, or other electronic or mechanical methods, without the prior written permission of the publisher, except in the case of brief quotations embodied in critical reviews and certain other noncommercial uses permitted by copyright law.

Cover and Interior Design by Charles Sheehan-Miles
Cover Photo by Erica Ritchie

DEDICATION

For Randall's Readers:

The swooniest, sexiest, smartest women (and men) around.

ACKNOWLEDGEMENTS

I WANT TO THANK the following kick-ass people:

Randall's Bitchin' Betas for their tireless work to help sharpen the story line and make this the best reading experience possible for you. Pamela Carrion, Laura Wilson, Sally Bouley, Lisa Rutledge, Stacey Grice, Lindsay Sparkes, Beth Suit, Erin Roth, and Erica Ritchie. You ladies are funny, fierce, and perfectly critical. Thank you for all of your had work!

Erica Ritchie for once again providing a fabulous photograph for cover use in this series. Check out her Facebook page, guys. She's a genius with that lens!

Charles Miles for your eyes, the cover design and interior design. But, most of all, thank you for making me want to write about weddings at all. Love you.

Finally, thank you to all of the readers of the November Blue Series, old and new, for supporting this project. I hope you enjoyed the ride, and are ready for the final installment of the series, "Bo & Ember," coming in April.

xo

CHAPTER ONE

BEST LAID PLANS

"IT WAS NEVER a question of *if* I was going to marry Ember, it was the matter of *when*. Five minutes after I met her may have been a bit hasty, but I swear to you that's how I felt. Like I wanted to sew her to my side and keep her there forever. We just ... went together." I took a deep breath, smiling at my words. Not because they were well-crafted, but because they were real. They were us.

I continued, reading from my composition notebook. "Then... some stuff happened. The kind of stuff that had the back of my mind questioning if we could really have a forever kind of life together. If we could really carry on an eternal relationship if the minutia of everyday life was bogging us down."

"Eeeerr!" Georgia made a very realistic—and very loud—buzzer sound with her voice. "Christ, Cavanaugh, are you trying to propose to her or serve her with divorce papers?"

We were in her bakery, she could talk to me however she wanted.

I looked to Regan, who covered his mouth, hiding a smile.

"Et tu, Regan?" I held out my arms, teasing him. "Shit, who am I kidding? That sucked."

I crumpled up the useless piece of paper and sat in the booth across from Regan and Georgia. We had one weekend off in between the two parts of our summer tour with The Six, and these precious minutes were few that I was able to steal away from Ember. We'd been on tour for weeks in the southern part of California, and after this weekend we'd be heading north. *Wine country,* Ember touted any time it was brought up.

Regan cleared his throat. "Let's, uh, take a look at what worked. That if and when statement? Perfection."

"Yeah, if he was proposing to every other girl on *Youtube* that got engaged this year. They all say that, Regan. Every single one of them. Shit, my Facebook feed blows up a few days a week with *oh so sweet! Look how much he loves her!* And, you know what? They all say 'I knew the second I met her,' or 'It was just a matter of time before I knew ...' Tell me, were you going to have Michael Bublé playing in the background?" She dramatically leaned her head back, pointing her index finger at her temple and pulling the imaginary trigger as her eyes rolled to the sky.

"I get it, I get it." Regan held up his hands. "Don't propose to Georgia on *Youtube*. Or with Michael Bublé playing in the background."

She shot up in her seat. "I didn't say that. Get your act together, Kane. Every girl wants to feel like a celebrity for five minutes of her life."

Regan held out his hands. "You're not making sense!"

"You act surprised!" she shot back, cracking into laughter right along side him.

Even though they'd only been together for a few months, Regan and Georgia had an easy banter between them. It was light and sarcastic and just what they both seemed to need.

I whistled and pointed to myself. "Help!" I pleaded. "I need to get this right."

"Right for who?" Georgia turned serious.

"Huh?" Regan and I said in unison.

Georgia leaned forward, placing her elbows on the table, and sliding a plate of cookies to the side. "Who do you want it to be right for? I mean, this is you two, right? I've only seen you guys in action for a couple of months, but you do things your own way. As it should be, don't get me wrong, but what's *right*?"

I leaned back with a heavy sigh. "I just want to marry her."

"So fuckin' marry her. She knows all of the shit you went through. God, even I know more than I need to about all of the shit you went through. She doesn't need to be reminded of that. She doesn't need to know what *happened*, she just needs to know why you want more. What you have planned for your future. Together. Just marry the girl and get on with it."

Unplanned and definitely uncool, Regan and I sniffed at the same time. Georgia rolled her eyes.

"God, let me out of this booth. I'll leave you ladies to it. Does anyone need a tampon while I'm up?" Georgia nudged Regan so she could get out.

She didn't wait for our response, instead making a beeline for the supplies in her kitchen. She started whipping up a batch of who-knows-what, though I knew it would be delicious. I watched Regan for a few moments as he stared at her.

"It's nice to see that look on your face, bro." I realized that adding "bro" to the end of the sentence didn't really beef it up any, but I let it hang there in the air.

He turned back to me, half grinning, half grey-looking. "It's not ... weird for you?"

I shook my head. It wasn't that I'd seen sparks between Georgia and Regan from the first minute. In fact, they'd both seemed to be doing their damnedest to stay away from each other. The more time they had spent together, though, it became clearer that he found peace with her.

As we sat in *Sweet Forty-Two*, in La Jolla, California, I found myself smiling. And not just from the permanent sugar high Georgia had me on.

"It's really not. It would be weird to me if you wallowed around all pale and mopey. Rae would think Georgia was a riot, which she is."

Regan swallowed hard. "It's been almost a year. Sometimes it feels like years ago, and sometimes it feels like we're still sitting on the floor of that hospital, doesn't it?"

My heart raced as I nodded my agreement. My sister had been gone for eleven months and four days. She and Regan had only been together for about two months, but he felt more like a brother to me than anyone else. I was glad when he decided to return to the US and maintain our friendship after his post-funeral hiatus from reality.

"It's bizarre. Do you still dream about her?" Admittedly, I'd been jealous when Regan was having frequent dreams about Rae. I didn't want to wake up screaming like he sometimes had, but I hadn't really dreamt about her at all—maybe one or two times—and I just wanted to see her once in a while. Hear her the way he could in his dreams.

"Sometimes," he conceded. "Less now than a few months ago, though."

I sighed. "Ember and her parents would ask if she ever said anything specific to you. You know, like it's actually *her* visiting you in your dreams."

Regan grinned. "Are you going to ask me that?"

I picked up a chocolate chip cookie and took a bite. "No. Not today, anyway."

"Can we talk about you asking the love of your life to spend the rest of it with you?"

"Argh," I groaned. "I'm a mess. I can verbalize awesome variations of my feelings to her on a whim. But, planned? Planned I just sound like some underprepared candidate."

"Have you called Monica?"

Oops.

Regan's eyes grew wide. "You haven't called Monica?"

"Who's Monica?" Georgia shouted from the kitchen as she slid a baking sheet into the oven.

"Ember's best friend. Like *best* friend." Regan darted his eyes between me and Georgia. "I only know that because of how Ember's droned on and on all summer about how I am *really great* to talk to, but she *needs* her best girlfriend. Not that I don't love listening to your girl, Bo, but damn can Monica talk. Is there a way to get her out here?"

I chuckled as Regan went off on his tangent. Regan and Ember had a great relationship that I was grateful for for both of their sakes.

Georgia walked into the cafe area, wiping her hands on her apron. "You dumb sack of shit. You haven't talked to her best friend? Whatever you do, don't tell her you already talked about this with someone else. She'll be offended."

"She will," Regan agreed. "I only know this because Ember, at one point, regaled the story of Josh and Monica's engagement to me, and mentioned not-so-kiddingly that she *forgave* Josh for not cluing her in."

Georgia snapped her fingers. "Both of you can it. Here comes Ember now." She tilted her head toward the door just as the sound of bells rang through the bakery.

"There you guys are!" Ember sounded breathless. "Anyone ever hear of answering their cell phones? Fuck!" She sat next to me, planting a chaste kiss on my cheek.

I grabbed her face and kissed her long and hard on the lips. I loved the little noise she made deep in her throat when I caught her off guard. "Hey you."

"Hey. Sorry for being all stormy there. I've just spent far too much fucking time with my mother today. Who doesn't like it when I swear. Fuck. Fuck, fuck fuck." Ember snatched a cookie off the plate and took half of it in one bite.

"Feel better?" Georgia quipped.

"Yes," Ember mumbled with a mouthful and pointed to the half cookie still in her hand. "Can we get some of these in our next order?"

Georgia nodded with a smile. "Your boyfriend already made sure of it."

By the time the summer tour with The Six started, *Sweet Forty-Two* was cranking in the orders. Georgia was flat out from the time she woke up at 4:00am until the door was locked at 6:00 in the evening. Before the tour had started, Regan lent a hand in the kitchen whenever he could. Once we left, though, she was on her own.

She sent us care packages every few days, whenever we got to a new location. Also, she closed the bakery on Wednesdays and Thursdays so she could catch up with us wherever we were. When we started the northern leg of our tour, it would be a little too far to drive, though.

"Will you be able to visit us at all during the next half of our tour?" Ember finished the cookie and looked to Georgia.

Georgia shrugged. "Depends. Are you guys going to be in Napa or Sonoma?"

"Both. I made sure we were booked there for extended dates," Ember said as if the decision was business-based and not grape-based.

"As long as you're not there over Labor Day weekend, when I've got a fuckload of orders, count me in." Georgia smiled, and went back into the kitchen when the timer on the oven dinged. Ember smiled back as I sighed a breath of relief at the possibility of *not* being forced to drink wine for three days straight.

Ember and Georgia had come a long way in their relationship over the last few months, as well. It was a rough go for the two of them, given the perceptions they each had about the other, and how protective Ember was of Regan.

"So why'd you track us down, Em? You seemed to be on a mission." Regan refocused the conversation.

"Oh, right," Ember grumbled. "Willow."

Regan and I groaned. The war of words between Willow and Ember was never ending. I knew Ember was struggling with the bombshell Willow had dropped on her months ago that she and Ember were actually biological half-sisters. That was Willow's statement, and not based on any facts we were aware of. It tore Ember up for a while, but she decided to put it on the back burner until we could all get through the tour and she could decide how she was going to approach her parents. Or if she was going to. Still, things were icy between the two former best friends, and Regan and I did our best to run interference as often as possible. Especially after Willow tried to make a pass at me earlier in the year.

"Keep it up, you guys. You'll really be moaning in a second. Get this. Willow will be joining us for the *entire* second half of the tour."

Georgia let out a sarcastic laugh from the kitchen, Regan thumped his forehead onto the table, and I screamed internally. Angry that my plans for a romantic proposal on the last night of the tour just got a little more complicated—if not impossible—with the unwelcome presence of Willow Shaw.

CHAPTER TWO

THE BEST FRIEND

"AND HOW'S MY favorite socialite-at-large?" Monica chirped playfully into the phone.

"Oh, *God*," I groaned.

Sometime shortly after Ember and I got together—the first time—Monica's background check led her to stumble upon an article in *The New Yorker* discussing my family's estate. The article was *supposed* to be about DROP, and it was—to some extent—but they seemed to err on the side of "Wealthy Eligible Bachelor Quietly Carries Out Family's Mission." She promised she'd never let me hear the end of it.

"Just kidding, don't get your money in a bunch. Anyway, it's about damn time you called me," she snapped. "This whole year I've heard *about* you from Ember and have seen texts you've sent Josh but ... me? Just forget about me, I guess."

"Sorry, Mon," I played along remorsefully.

"Oh no you don't, mister. You don't get to call me *Mon* until you grovel."

"I want to marry Ember." The words tumbled out like Yahtzee dice.

Silence.

"Groveling over," Monica said flatly. "Tell me everything."

"That ... is everything." I looked around the beach that called itself my back yard. "You can't tell her, Monica. I'm serious. Regan and Georgia said I had to call—"

"Regan and who did what? Others know?"

Shit. I'd been instructed—by Georgia nonetheless—not to say anything to Monica about her knowledge. Fail.

"I ... I was just talking to them about the speech ..." I trailed off.

Monica snorted into the phone. "With any luck they told you to ditch the speech all together. You know better, Cavanaugh. Come on, where's your A-game?" She sounded like my high school football coach.

"I don't know what I'm doing. I don't want it to be cliché, but I want it to be special. Ember's—"

"Stop," she cut me off again. "Slow your roll and just breathe."

I took a deep breath, chuckling a little at the end of it.

"Something funny?" Monica questioned.

"So you, Regan, and Georgia all know that I want to propose to her and no one has batted an eyelash about the fact that we've only been together for just over a year, and that includes a long ... break." I winced as I said it. Ember and I rarely, if ever, discussed the time we'd spent *not* together. It was a hiccup. That's how we referred to it.

"No one's batted an eyelash because even relative strangers can tell how in love you ar. Remember, you yourself said *a thousand lifetimes.*"

For as long as she lived, Monica would never let me—or Josh—forget what she called the most romantic words she'd ever heard uttered from another human's mouth. Sometimes she'd tease Josh for not saying them himself to her, and he'd call me an asshole for saying it at all.

She was right, though. I hadn't worried much about the actual time we'd been together, because it was like our souls were joined long before our bodies ever met.

"I want you to be there," I said. "While it'll be about me and Ember, I want all the people she loves there. I want the whole thing to be about love."

"Of course you do!" Josh shouted from somewhere in the background.

"Am I on speakerphone?" I nearly shouted.

"Uh ..." Monica stammered.

I laughed. "You guys are a piece of work."

"Do you think you'll be ready by the last week in August? We just booked our tickets to come out while you guys are playing in Napa."

My palms started to sweat, but my words highlighted the truth. "I've been ready since I first kissed her, Monica."

"I know you have, Bo. Just keep your cool until then. Whatever you do, do *not* ask her dad for permission until, like, right before you do it."

Her suggestion took me by surprise. "Seriously?"

"My God," she said, sounding frustrated, "the man can *not* keep a secret to save his life. That info will serve you well around her birthday, too. He totally blew the surprise twenty-first I'd spent a semester planning. He's just so *enthusiastic* about life that he can't contain his little self."

I laughed at full-volume. Ember's dad was the full-on embodiment of a peaceful, hippie dad. He was super involved, über sensitive, and I could almost picture him helping Ember get ready for prom.

"Thanks for the heads up." That was precisely why Georgia said to call the best friend, I realized.

"Just keep your hat on for another five weeks. Do you think you can do that?" Monica's tone was calm, which I apparently needed as my palms continued to sweat.

"Will do."

I hung up with Monica, tossed my phone on the bed, and wiped my hands on my jeans.

"Who were you on the phone with?" Ember slowly opened the bedroom door and my stomach dropped, wondering both when she'd gotten home and how much she'd heard.

"Josh," I said causally. It was the closest thing to a non-lie I could come up with. If I'd said *Monica* she would have known something was up.

"Oh! Did he tell you they're able to come out for the Napa show?" Ember's eyes lit up like they hadn't in a long time. I hadn't been conscious of how long it had been since I'd seen her so lively until she smiled like that.

I held out my hands, leading her to me. "He did. You seem really happy."

Ember folded herself perfectly into my embrace as she sighed into my chest. "I haven't seen her since January. It's the longest we've ever gone without seeing each other since college, for God's sake."

I rested my chin on the top of her head, rubbing her back. "I know Regan and I are certainly no substitute for Monica."

"I didn't mean it like that." Ember shook her head as she pulled back.

"Oh, neither did I. I was serious. Sometimes I have no idea what the hell to say to you, and I wish I could have a hotline to Monica to ask. Really. I'm glad she's coming."

Ember rested her head on my shoulder. "Everything with Willow ... and now she's coming with us on tour ..."

While Willow was an integral part of the recording of our album, her skills were studio based and not needed on the tour. The first half of the tour had given Ember a lot of breathing room from Willow and the dark cloud she carried around with her. Willow herself was always in a good mood, but that seemed to be at the expense of others, and, frankly, I was glad to have her out of my hair for a while, too.

Despite the fact that I shook off her advances a few months ago, Willow kept an uncomfortable eye on me. She made sure Ember never saw it, and I'd certainly never draw Ember's attention to it, but I wasn't looking forward to dodging those glances again.

"Why is she coming?" I finally asked.

"To ruin my life." Ember tucked a heavy blanket of sarcasm around her words. "She wants to *see Napa*," she cooed like a child, mocking the light and airy way Willow produced her words. "As if she hasn't spent *significant* amounts of time there since she turned twenty-one. God, she's annoying."

"We won't let her ruin it." I tried to sound encouraging, but my nerves surrounding my own plans for Napa were getting in the way.

Ember looked up at me with her gorgeous jade-colored eyes. "You're right. The more I let her get to me, the more she'll try."

I laughed. "You know what? Do you want to get away for the weekend?"

"Away? That's where we've been all summer. *Away*. Where do you propose we go?"

I snatched my cell from the bed, and led Ember by the hand through our beachfront condo. When I reached the counter in the kitchen, I picked up Ember's phone, too.

"What are you doing?" She asked.

I continued leading her around as I formulated the plan in my head. I reached the front door and let go of Ember's hand as I locked the dead bolt. Though I was no longer holding her hand, she continued to follow my path. Walking to the sliding glass doors, I locked those and pulled the blinds, turning them so they blocked out all sunlight. I did that with each window I passed, too. Finally, I made sure to lock the back door by the garage. Once we finished the circle around the house, I led us back into our bedroom, where I removed the batteries from our phones, and tucked them into the top drawer of the dresser.

"Here." I shut the bedroom door and locked it, pulling Ember into a kiss.

"I beg your pardon?" she asked when she pulled away.

"Let's hide out here all weekend. We know when we have to leave on Monday, and everyone told everyone else to leave them alone all weekend. You know Georgia and Regan will be unavailable, and everyone else is catching up on sleep. Stay here with me for the whole weekend, Ember."

The corners of her mouth lifted slowly into a smile. "Bo, I'll stay anywhere you want me to, and for a hell of a lot longer than a weekend."

As she pressed her lips into mine, sliding her hands up the back of my shirt, I hoped that in a few weeks she'd say *yes* to forever.

"Forever?" I led her toward the bed, pulling my shirt over my head as she leaned back on the mattress. The word came out at the end of my thought, but we'd toyed with the word so often since we'd been together it wasn't out of place.

"Longer," she whispered back, pulling me down on top of her.

It was all I could do to stop myself from proposing to her right there. Asking her to be my wife, my partner for as long as eternity lasted. I took a breath and realized that a proposal was far below what I was planning for us.

For us, it really was forever. And it needed to start at the exact moment we were both ready. I'd make sure that moment was under starlight in Napa.

CHAPTER THREE

LOCKDOWN

"Do you think anyone will get worried?" Ember rolled over, her soft skin brushing against mine as she set her chin on my chest. "I mean, we've all been up each other's asses all summer …"

I laughed, running my fingers through her hair and down her back to her waist. "They know where to find us if there's an emergency, Em. Your parents live two houses down."

That was a thought I tried to keep buried deep in the back of my brain whenever I made love to their daughter.

Ember sat up and straddled my waist, anchoring one knee on each side of my hips. "It hadn't really occurred to me before the start of the tour how little privacy we'd have." She leaned forward and kissed my nose, then my mouth, then worked her lips down my jaw and neck.

"True. Two RVs don't really scream romance, do they?" My voice had stayed steady until Ember's mouth touched down on my chest, and she started moving her hips.

"And the day after tomorrow, we'll have to be around all of those old hippies who have *zero* problem with romance in an RV."

I laughed even though it was the last thing I wanted to do as Ember shifted down my body, her mouth working lower down my torso. "Well, maybe we'll have to give those old married hippies a run for their money."

"Ew, Bo!" Ember sat up and slapped my chest. "My *parents are* those people!"

"Don't remind me!" I laughed, sitting up and rolling her over. When she was beneath me, I brushed her wild auburn waves from her face. "We'll be there someday, too, you know."

"Where?" She started moving those mouth watering hips under me.

"Old. Married. Maybe not hippies. Well, I'll save that title for you," I teased.

"Well, my parents aren't *actually* married, I don't think. Unless they did that sometime when I wasn't looking." She shrugged and leaned up to kiss me, but I pulled back.

"What?"

Her eyes moved from side to side. "What?"

"Your parents aren't married?"

"Why are you acting so surprised?"

I opened and closed my mouth several times, but nothing worth saying came out.

"What's the big deal?" She asked, sitting up against the headboard as I stared into space.

"Isn't ... marriage a big deal? Didn't it ever bother you when you were little?"

She grinned and moved to cross her legs. I sat back. "I didn't know it wasn't normal, Bo. Sure, I attended lots of commitment ceremonies and things like that when I was little, but ..." she trailed off and shrugged. "It just wasn't a *thing*. Some people were married, some weren't, but most were committed, you know? I knew my parents were together, and in it forever, so *married* didn't hold any significance."

"Does it now?" My throat ran dry. The shock here wasn't that Ember's parents weren't married. Once I'd thought about it for a second, I realized how in step with their lifestyle that was. I realized we'd never even discussed marriage. It was lots of *lifetimes* and *eternities,* but *marriage* hadn't been verbalized.

"I think marriage is great, if that's what people want. Josh and Monica, for example. I was a mess when he proposed. Those two *needed* to be married, like, immediately." She laughed softly and moved her hands to my thighs. I placed my hands over her wrists.

"I mean does it hold significance to *you*?" I spoke firmly but still quietly. Her eyes met mine with confusion but it slowly registered as her lips parted with a click of her tongue and a sigh.

"I haven't really ..."

"Thought about it?" I cut her off. "Are you kidding?"

"Well, no, I mean ... Yes, I've thought about it because I knew your parents were married—or at least I assumed they were—and most people prioritize marriage." Her cheeks were growing pink, right about the rate at which my stomach sank.

"Most people? Like, people who aren't you?" I didn't mean the irritation in my voice, but it was hard to contain.

"What's the big deal? I'm not saying that to be passive but, for Christ's sake, Bo, I want to be with you for-*ever*, what does a piece of paper have to do with that?"

I exhaled roughly, swinging my legs over the edge of the bed. "It matters because it's a rite of passage with the person you love. That you put on that *piece of paper* that you *promise* forever. It's written."

"Soooo my words don't hold enough weight unless they're printed?" Ember drew her eyebrows together as she put her feet on the floor, following the walk I'd decided to take through the bedroom door.

"I don't want to fight." I ran a hand through my hair, entering the kitchen and pulling a bottle of Vitamin Water out of the fridge.

"Who's fighting?" Ember looked around, her tone careful.

I gulped the water until half the bottle was gone, then slammed it down on the counter.

"That was a little aggressive." Ember crossed her arms and arched her eyebrow.

"Marry me," I blurted out.

Her nostrils flared as her face twisted in pure sarcastic splendor. "I was wrong ... *that* was aggressive."

"You don't want to marry me?" Sweat sprang up on the back of my neck. This wasn't how I was supposed to ask her to marry me, but she wasn't supposed to not answer, either.

"You've lost your goddamn mind, Bo. You're not asking me to marry you right now. You're freaking the fuck out and it's not okay." She placed her hands on her hips and swallowed hard.

"What if I was?"

"What if you were what?"

I took a deep breath through my nose. "What if I was asking you to marry me right now?"

Ember rolled her eyes. "You're not, though."

My voice grew dark. "Answer the question, Ember."

"I—"

I didn't let her finish before I cut her off by holding up my hand.

I bit my lip. I didn't want to yell, but I didn't want to stand in the room with her anymore. That was more my fault than hers. She had no way of knowing that with every word she spoke she was spearing every plan I had for us for the rest of the summer ... and the rest of our lives. As I headed for the door, Ember seemed to sense what I was doing, and beat me to it, placing her hand on the knob.

"No way," she nearly yelled, her eyes fierce with passion. "Hiding out here all weekend, remember?" She pressed her back against the door, blocking my exit.

I rolled my eyes. "I can just go out the back door, Ember."

"Right. But you won't, because you're not an asshole. You're not going to run away from this conversation by accusing me of running away from it, Bo."

Her eyes widened as tears threatened to fall, and her cheeks were still red. Even worse, she was right. The good news was, she wanted me to stay, even though I was acting like a total ass.

"Okay." I sighed. "Sorry. So ... what do we do?"

Relief spread across her face. "Well, we dial down the panic a notch." She walked past me, toward the oversized couch where she curled herself up.

"Yeah." I chuckled nervously as I walked to the living space and sat next to her.

"So, do you want to talk about the whole marriage thing?" She lifted her eyebrows and twisted her lips playfully.

"No," I said, surprising myself.

Ember leaned into me, pulling my arm way from my body and wrapping it around her shoulders as she snuggled into my chest. The smell of lemongrass was never far away. I kissed the top of her head and took a deep breath, grateful that I didn't have to have a conversation with Ember about her thoughts on marriage to know … to know that soon I'd ask her to be my wife … and she'd say yes.

"Can I interest you in a topic change?" Ember's voice lowered at the end of her sentence. She moved her lips to my neck and left them there until I responded.

"Anything you want."

Her grin excited me. *"Anything?"*

I nodded, and all the blood my brain needed to process an answer raced south.

Ember pulled away from my body, throwing her hair up into a loose ponytail.

"What are you doing?" I asked as she worked her hands across the belt of my shorts.

"I want to see you the whole time. And I want you to see me." After she undid my zipper, she lifted her shirt over her head, tossing it behind her where it landed on the coffee table.

I slid my shorts off as she stepped out of her long skirt. She stood in front of me for a moment, while I took off my shirt, and I could barely complete that task while staring at her form. The way her waist curved in, leaving soft slender hips in their wake, stole my breath. The sliver of a shadow her breasts created over her ribs begged me to touch her. With her hair pulled back, I had the good fortune of viewing the length of her, from her flawless hair that hung down past her breasts, all the way to her toes. Unobstructed.

"I can't have you standing that far from me anymore," I whispered, the obvious physical sign of my readiness posted up between us. She held out her hand as I reached for her, allowing me to pull her on top of me.

Hovering over me, her knees digging into the couch, she paused, drawing her lips across my jawline and ending at my ear so she could whisper to me. "I've never wanted anyone as badly as I want you at this moment."

Her hard nipples pressed against my chest and I wrapped my hands around her hips. "So what are you going to do about it?" I growled into her ear.

Challenge flickering in her eyes, Ember moved her hands to the tops of my shoulders and slowly slid onto me. Excruciatingly slow. My fingers dug into her skin as she exhaled loudly, throwing her head back.

Each time we made love, I had to spend the first few seconds getting a grip or I feared it would end right there. The way she overrode my well trained sexual defenses caught me off guard more than I cared to admit. All guys have them ... things they think about when they don't want the sex to be over in a split second. Mine ranged from sports to standing naked in a blizzard. It's true.

Somehow, though, when Ember tilted her chin back down and stared at me with warm devotion, that was all the focus I needed. I wanted her. Needed her. Wanted her to feel everything I felt in this moment.

"What?" She whispered, breathless as she moved against me.

I shook my head, moving my hand to the back of her neck, where I tugged on her elastic and released her hair. A forest of soft auburn encircled us in an instant.

"What are you doing?" She insisted, moving faster.

I gripped her harder, allowing the silk of her hair to tickle the side of my neck. "I want to be swallowed by you."

I pulled down on her hips harder, and she answered by moving faster, pressing her forehead into my shoulder as I groaned through clenched teeth.

"Ah," she cried out in that quick, panicked, high-pitched way that told me she was close.

"Open your eyes," I commanded, my words spilling out in disorganized ecstasy.

Ember lifted her head, her pupils overtaking her eyes. As they rested on mine for a few seconds, I felt the tension building in the way her movements became less graceful. More staggered. More desperate.

"I'm …" Ember trailed off as she clenched around me, pulsing hard and fast. Her eyes stayed on me for a few seconds before she threw her head back once more, calling my name over and over as her voice bounced off the walls of our house.

Normally I can enjoy the fullness of her orgasm before I'm brought to my own. Not this time. Between the high anxiety I'd been dealing with over proposing to her, and nearly blowing that all up earlier, and the way her chest heaved under her breaths, I couldn't hold on anymore.

I thrusted her down, wrapping my arms around her and pulling her tightly to me as I buried my face in her neck. Her orgasm continued to move through her as mine came. We moaned and panted together as our bodies came to rest and the only thing I could hear was the desire in my heart for this amazing woman. One who I desperately wanted to call my wife.

CHAPTER FOUR

TICK, TICK TICK ...

DESPITE MY EARLY efforts to screw myself over completely, Ember and I enjoyed the weekend the way we'd intended to. Emotionally far away from everyone else in The Six, we only left the bed to go to the bathroom, or move to the couch. It seemed like a good idea at the time to have my girlfriend naked all weekend. That is until Monday morning came and we were shoulder to shoulder with her parents and all of their friends.

"You look as worn out as I feel." Regan spoke dryly as we loaded gear under the bus for leg number two of our summer tour.

"If I look anything like you do, Kane, kill me now." I laughed as I slammed one of the compartments shut on the large RV.

From the depths of sarcasm rose Georgia in a fluttery mock-Southern accent. "Why, *no one* could possibly ever look like you do, Bo Cavanaugh. You're just a dream, wrapped in a milkshake, dipped in—"

"Okay, okay we get it. He's *super hot*," Regan exaggerated while shaking his head.

Georgia lifted way up onto her tip-toes. "*You're* super hot," she whispered into his ear before she kissed it.

Just after Georgia waved goodbye and Regan wiped the smirk from his face, the RVs were loaded and we were waiting for a few stragglers. Namely, Willow.

Ember marched down the stairs of the lead vehicle. "Are we set? I heard the doors underneath close."

"Just waiting for Willow," Regan rattled off.

Ember looked between the two of us, took a deep breath, and walked slowly back into the RV.

"That could have gone worse." Regan sounded relieved as he patted my shoulder.

"I just hope she's not saving it for when she sees Willow face-to-face." By avoiding the rest of the band all weekend, we'd also managed to avoid talk of the overly sexualized flower-child arch nemesis.

Regan adjusted the straps on his backpack as he slid his sunglasses on. "It can't be any worse than Willow trying to hit on you, right?" His tone was hopeful as he smiled.

"Let's hope not," I groaned and followed Regan onto the RV, where Ember had cleared space for the three of us to sit.

"Hey, where are they going?" Ember shouted up to her dad, who was at the wheel, as she pointed out the window. The second RV in our tiny caravan was pulling out of the parking lot.

Ashby addressed Ember through the rearview mirror. "They've got to get gas. We'll catch up with them when Willow gets here."

Regan and I shot each other a look.

"She's riding in here?" Ember cleared her throat, her new tactic for avoiding a nasty tone in her voice when she *really* wanted to deliver one.

"That's not going to be a problem, is it, dear? We all thought you two girls could use some time together to ... get over ... whatever the heck is going on." Raven didn't look up as she paged her way through a paperback. There was nothing on the cover but abs and a guitar. I assume there was a title, but even I couldn't see one through the expertly organized masculinity.

I held my breath. I was certain Ember wouldn't tell her parents about Willow's accusation that she and Ember were half sisters, but her mother's casual attitude about their apparent rivalry was bound to make Ember's head explode one of these days.

"It's not a problem for me," Ember asserted. "Does Willow know she'll be cozy with us for the next several hours, at the very least?"

"Let's find out, shall we?" Ashby said with a smile as he opened the RV door for Willow, who bounded up the steps with much more pep than awaited her in the cabin of the vehicle.

"Hey, guys ..." Her brightness slid away with her words as she looked at Ember.

Before any of us had a chance to say anything, there was a loud pounding on the door.

Just behind Willow marched a much shorter, and much louder, Georgia. Willow turned to face her, having to look down to meet Georgia's eyes. That didn't seem to affect Georgia as she pointed emphatically at Willow.

"Listen here," she spoke to Willow without so much as looking in our direction, laying on her thickest Eastern Massachusetts accent, "we both know the kind of shit you pull. We also know you won't be pulling that with Regan, correct?"

"Excuse—" Willow started, but was cut off.

"Correct?" Georgia stepped up one more stair so she was as close as she was going to get to Willow's eye-line.

"Whatever," Willow mumbled as she slumped down in her seat right behind Ashby.

"Will that be all, Georgia?" Ashby arched the eyebrow he'd passed down to Ember.

She smiled and kissed him on the cheek. "You betchya, Mr. Harris. Bye guys! See you in a few weeks!" She waved frantically at us for a second before bounding off the bus and back to her car.

The RV was silent with the precise tension that fills a high school classroom after a clashing of the social groups. I thought, based on Willow's initial silence, that we'd successfully passed through level one unscathed.

I was wrong.

Ember's shoulders rose with a huge breath as Willow stood and walked with an inappropriately seductive grin to the back of the vehicle.

"Don't worry," Willow said, smiling at Regan as she sat next to him across the table from Ember and me. "You're not really my type. No offense."

"None taken." Regan pulled his Kindle out of his backpack and diverted his attention from the table.

"Doing anyone and everyone isn't really a type, Willow." Ember pulled her iPod from her bag, plugged in her earbuds, and leaned her head back as she closed her eyes.

A flash of homicidal irritation passed through Willow's eyes before she turned her gaze to me. And grinned.

"Not *everyone*," she whispered.

I held my face steady enough as she rose from the table and walked back to her seat.

I exhaled once I was sure Willow was securely fastened somewhere far from me. Regan shook his head and lifted his eyes from his reading. "Good fuckin' luck, dude."

"Thanks," I murmured.

Let me be clear. There wasn't one ounce of anything I found attractive about Willow Shaw. Sure, she was visually attractive, but the venom that appeared to course through her body erased it all, and then some. The problem, it seemed, was that she wasn't going to give up. I hoped that stunt she pulled was more in response to feeling burned by Georgia, and not any lingering game she saw in me.

* * *

"Bo ... Bo ..." A sickeningly familiar voice called me from the pleasant nap I'd been enjoying. As consciousness overtook me, I realized the RV had stopped. Looking to my left, out the window, I saw we were at a park and some of the band members were eating at nearby picnic tables.

I didn't want to look right. I knew who was there, and I didn't want to acknowledge her. Sitting up, I rubbed the sleep from my eyes, wondering where Ember was, and why the hell she'd leave Willow in the RV with me.

Looking up, I indeed saw Willow, who was sitting in the chair across the aisle from the table I'd been napping at. Her legs were crossed at the knee, and her foot bobbed softly as she sat with her arms crossed.

I cleared my throat while I sat up. "Where is everyone?"

She nodded her head to the windows. "Eating. Stretching."

"K ..." I took a deep breath and slid out of the bench seat, standing in the aisle, stretching once more.

I felt her eyes on me as I made my way toward the door. You'd think I would breathe a sigh of relief as I saw Ember approach the RV. You'd be wrong. Just as I reached the top of the stairs, Ember pushed past me and headed straight for Willow.

"What the hell are you doing in here?" She yelled, causing the hair on the back of my neck to stand up.

Willow's voice was maniacally even. "What? You don't trust your *soul mate*?" The sarcasm around the term threw Ember into a rage. I turned around and walked quickly back to the quarrel.

Ember's hands flew everywhere as she screamed some more. "I don't trust *you*! You've already tried to put your slutty hands all over him once, and I'll be damned if you try again. He's too much of a gentleman to tell you to fuck off, but I'm not."

Willow thrusted her hands forward, aiming for Ember's hair, but Ember stuck her arm up. The cracking of skin sent me forward, and I wrapped my arm around Ember's waist, pulling her back as she lunged forward.

"Are you kidding me? You were going to slap me? Slap me, then! Do it! I fucking *dare* you, Willow. Slap me."

I spun Ember around, so I was standing between the mortal enemies, my ears fielding obscenities from both sides.

"Guys, stop!" I yelled. A completely futile effort on my part as words shot through and around me, and hands grabbed at whatever they could.

Willow's eyes were black with rage as her lip curled with each perfectly crafted insult.

"You're a spoiled little daddy's girl who can't handle when she loses."

Ember scrunched her face as she growled. Growled. "I'm spoiled? I'm spoiled?! You're the one who grew up with her daddy's *trust fund* behind every school you were admitted to, before you were kicked out!"

What seemed like a full minute later—and a minute is a long time when you're in the middle of a bonafied cat fight—Regan raced up the stairs.

"What the fuck?" He held out his hands, seeming to feel as helpless as I probably looked.

"Get her out!" I nodded to Ember, who was closest to the door, as I held Willow back with my forearm.

I breathed half a sigh of relief as Regan squatted down and hoisted a flailing Ember over his shoulder.

"Let me down, Regan! This isn't funny!"

"No shit it's not funny, you've lost your head. Shut up and stop moving so we both don't fall down the stairs." Their voices trailed off as I remained planted in the RV, and saw the rest of the group and crew moving toward the vehicle.

Oh good. A full-blown scene.

"You can put your arm down, you know." Willow spoke as if nothing had happened, though I could still her ragged breath between her words.

I turned slowly, my eyes nearly bulging out of my head. "You need to get it together." Those were the only words that I spoke before dropping my guard and walking off the RV, to a still enraged Ember.

"November Blue, get ahold of yourself." Ashby grabbed his daughter's shoulders as they moved up and down against deep breaths.

Raven moved to my side. "What happened?" Her look was slightly suspicious, and I couldn't really blame her given the undercurrent to the girls' relationship, but I was still slightly offended.

"Nothing to do with me, Raven." I shook my head, annoyed.

She sighed and said, "Of course not, that's not what I meant."

It was, but I let it slide. We were all human in our thinking, after all.

The muscles in my back froze as I heard the measured steps of Willow making her way off the RV.

Finally, Ember spoke as she pointed to the pot-stirrer who had her arms crossed as she stood just to my side.

"Her. She *happened*," Ember seethed as she crossed to come face to face with Willow. It was kind of like watching a predator and prey in the wild, though none of us knew who was which at the moment, so we stood still. On alert.

"Girls," Solstice, Willow's mother who was normally ethereal and quiet, cut her words through the awkward silence. "Enough is enough."

"This has gone on long enough," Michael added.

I noticed that Mags and Journey were hanging back, watching the scene carefully, as though it were a series of whipping live wires.

Raven sounded flustered as she threw her hands in the air. "If this has nothing to do with Bo, then I demand you two spill what it is that has you at each other's throats."

Oh, God ...

Regan and I looked at each other, his face paling as his eyes grew wide. Ember and Willow turned, facing each other with their hands on their hip as if they were silently daring each other to say it.

Just when I thought one of them had come up with a fabulous lie, Ember slowly lifted her chin and turned to face the band.

"For months ... *months* ... Willow has *insisted* that she and I are sisters. Half sisters. I've told her to drop it a thousand times, and she won't. Now is a good a time as any to put it to rest, don't you think."

Ember tucked her hair behind her ears, and I watched a tear roll down Solstice's cheek.

"Mom," Willow spoke with the vulnerability of a lost toddler. "I'm right, aren't I?"

Ember snapped. "Come on, you're completely ridiculous."

At once, Raven moved to Ashby's side, and Michael clutched Solstice's hand. They all looked at each other in a way that made me move to Ember and grab her hand. She looked up at me with the hope of the last few months shattered in her eyes.

Solstice cleared her throat. "She's right ... Willow is right."

CHAPTER FIVE

BOOM

THE WORDS "WILLOW'S right" dropped like an atom bomb over the group as we stood in a gorgeous, unassuming park in Northern California. Out of the corner of my eye, I watched Journey and Mags turn and walk back to their picnic blanket, never once looking over their shoulder. Regan looked like he didn't know what to do, but being the kind of guy he is, he stepped closer to me and Ember. From just behind me I heard the release of Willow's tears. Stranded and alone against the side of the RV as her parents walked around us to get to her.

Parents.

Ember stared at hers, then moved her gaze to Willow.

"No." Ember shook her head, and I could feel the muscles trembling in her hands. "No ..."

"Sweetie," Raven let go of Ashby's hand and stepped toward Ember, who took a step back.

"Then who…if we're…who is…no…"

"Girls," Michael spoke with his arm around Willow. "We should talk about this inside." He nodded to the RV and led Willow and his wife up the stairs.

"Let's go," Ashby whispered, placing his arm around Ember's shoulders.

"No ... no ..." Ember was in a daze, her tone getting angrier by the moment.

I kissed her temple and gave her hand a soft squeeze. "I'll be right here when you come out."

She whipped her head around, staring at me in apparent fear. "You're not coming?"

My eyes moved over the fragile family, and I stroked Ember's cheek with my thumb. "This is between you and them, okay? I'll literally be standing *right* here when you come out."

Ember leaned against Ashby's body as he led her up the stairs into the RV. Raven mouthed a grateful "thank you" to me as she followed the pair, shutting the door behind her.

As soon as they were out of sight, I rubbed my hand over my mouth, leaving it there as I took a deep breath.

"Shit," I mumbled with my hand still over my mouth.

Regan let out a heavy breath. "Yeah ... shit. Want to go for a walk, or something?"

I shook my head. "I told her I'd be here when they were done."

"It could take forever."

"Yep."

Regan nodded and posted up next to me. "So, what ... the hell? Ember looks exactly like her mom, and Willow looks like *her* mom."

I turned my head, watching Regan play DNA connect-the-dots in his head.

I shrugged. "And, it doesn't help that Ashby and Michael kind of look alike. Not like brothers, but maybe cousins ... God, I don't know. Suddenly I can't remember what the hell anyone looks like." I squatted down on my heels and Regan followed.

"They have the same exact eyes." He sat all the way on the ground, resting his hands behind him as he stretched his legs out in front of him.

"Ember and Willow?"

His eyebrows shot up. "You've never noticed?"

I sighed, sinking my body onto the loose gravel at the edge of the parking lot. "It was the first thing I noticed when I met Willow for the first time last year. It startled me, honestly. To see the first thing I ever noticed about November mirrored back on the face of a childhood friend of hers? Jesus ..."

"It's not just the color, either. It's the shape, the way they sit on their faces ..." Regan trailed off.

"This isn't good." My mouth dried at the implications.

Regan sat forward, bending his knees. "So ... that means one of them grew up with a dad that wasn't their biological dad, then, right?"

The thought speared me in a way I hadn't felt pain in a long time. Ember and her dad had an amazing relationship. It was peaceful and respectful, a silent harmony always flowing between them.

"That's why Ember never wanted to talk about it. I mean, Christ, Regan, we talk about *everything* and she didn't even want to talk about this. Not one sentence. There was nothing I could do to even ease into the conversation."

"Do you think she knew?"

I shrugged and shook my head. "I have no fucking idea. I honestly think she didn't even want to think about it. For months this has been bubbling under the surface. Fuck, I want to ask this woman to marry me and I can't even get her to talk about something this big?" My heart raced. I couldn't reach Ember about this. She kept me away. I wondered if she was still going to push me away when she walked out of that RV.

From behind me, soft footsteps carried a softer voice. "You guys will be okay. This will be okay." Mags brushed her fingertips along my back as she and Journey sat on either side of me.

"I'm gonna call Georgia. I'll be back in a bit." Regan stood, brushing dust from his jeans as he walked away.

I could hardly blame him for needing some space from the conversation, and I respected his desire to give me privacy, but I could have used a little assistance with the Hippie Peace Force that surrounded me.

"Do you want to take a walk, too?" Journey nudged my arm with her elbow.

Mags looked around me to her parter. "He told November he'd be right here when she came out." She planted a soft kiss on my cheek. "I think that's sweet."

"It's necessary. Did you two know anything?"

Mags looked to the sky as Journey let out a slight sigh.

Fantastic.

"Come on, Mags," I pleaded.

Mags ran her hand over her short brown hair, stopping it at the back of her neck. When she looked at me, her large brown eyes were uncertain. "It's not my story to tell, Bo."

As a matter of course, I looked to Journey for a second opinion. Her blonde dreadlocks moved slowly as she shook her head in apology.

I was growing annoyed—and more anxious—as the minutes passed, though I was sure they felt longer inside that RV than out where I was sitting. "Fine. If you two don't mind, I'd rather wait here alone."

Without another word, the couple stood and wandered through two thick trees and into an open field far from the RV. Every other second, or so, I wanted to bail from my post and join them in the sun. In a world that existed only an hour before. The world where Ember knew where she came from. Given the unrest Ember discussed in her childhood—always moving from place to place—she always said that her family was what anchored her. I didn't know what was going on inside that RV, but I readied the rowboat anyway.

＊＊

A few hours passed before any signs of life came from the RV. Regan had returned earlier, but grabbed my guitar from underneath the vehicle and posted up under a tree a couple hundred feet away, toying with the strings. At some point, Journey and Mags made their way back to the second RV in our dysfunctional caravan, and I hadn't seen them in two hours.

My legs were alternating between burning and falling asleep when the door opened. In a second I shot to my feet, regretting the hasty movement as my legs woke angrily. With grace on my side, Ember was the first out of the RV. There wasn't anything in my emotional history that could have prepared me for what awaited.

With swollen eyes, red splotches across her paler cheeks, and her hair tied back from her face, Ember moved slowly down the stairs. The sounds from my guitar ceased from behind me, as Regan appeared to be taking in the scene.

I stepped toward her and held out my hand. When she reached me she didn't look up. She simply took my hand and started walking toward the far end of the parking lot.

"We're renting a car and driving to the next venue." Her voice was hoarse and further away than I'd ever heard. She didn't try to clear her throat as she continued. "You and I are driving to the rest of the tour dates, okay? I've called the car company and they'll be here in twenty minutes. Can you get our things?"

I stopped us at the edge of the grass and grabbed her shoulders, turning her to face me. When she still wouldn't look up, I lifted her chin with my fingers. Reluctantly, her eyes moved to mine.

"Ember," I whispered. "What happened?"

Without hesitation, her face melted into a torrent of tears. Words stumbled out fragmented between sobs. "Just ... just get the stuff, okay?"

I pulled her to me, holding her head to my chest, still left with as many questions as I had hours earlier. When her cries quieted, I kissed the top of her head. "I'll be right back."

Ember nodded and wiped her face dry as she turned her back. "I'm going to freshen up in the restroom." She spoke softly without turning around.

As I walked back to the RV, I watched Willow exit with her parents and move to the other RV. I hadn't seen Raven or Ashby yet, but I was about to since I needed to get our things from inside the vehicle.

Not knowing the protocol for such a thing, I rapped my knuckles against the side of the open door. "It's just Bo ... I'm ... coming to get our stuff."

I walked the rest of the way and found Raven and Ashby sitting silently at the table that just this morning held the laughter of me and my friends.

"Of course, Bo. Come on in." Raven tried a smile, but it barely spread across her entire mouth before disappearing.

I pulled our backpacks down from the overhead cabinet, and stuffed them with our phones and iPod's and other things we'd strewn around as we'd made ourselves comfortable for what was to be a long drive. Asbhy and Raven remained silent.

"So …" I started, feeling more awkward around Ember's parents than I ever had. Especially since I wasn't sure if I was looking at *both* of Ember's parents. "Ash, can you just … give me the names of the next few venues so I can program the addresses in my phone?"

Ashby stood, his thick greying hair sticking up as though he'd raked his hand through it one too many times. "Of course."

He moved to the front of the vehicle, and I followed, glancing back over my shoulder in time to see Raven rest her head against the window with her eyes closed.

"Here you go, son." Ashby handed me a sheet with the list of our tour dates, venues, and times.

It was then that he met my eyes. Water worn and tired, a flicker of Ember passed through them that had me more confused than ever. I wanted answers, but wanted them from Ember.

"Thanks. We'll see you in San Francisco. Drive safely." I turned on my heels, not knowing what else to say or do.

"Bo?" Ashby called after me.

I turned back around to find the broken smile of a kind man. "Take care of her okay?"

I nodded. "Always."

Regan was waiting, leaning against the RV as I planted my feet on the ground.

"Is everything ... you're not leaving the tour are you?"

"God, no. Thankfully. At least, that's not the plan right now. We're driving." I nodded to the far end of the parking lot where I watched Ember climb into the driver's seat of the rental car that must have shown up while I was inside.

"I ... so ... Ember's my friend, and so are you, but I'm thinking you two should drive alone for a while? Right?" His eyebrows twisted as he struggled to find the words.

I chuckled. "That'd be great, man. Trust me, I want you with us as much as I'm sure Ember does, but I still don't know what the hell happened there. We'll see you in San Fran tonight."

Regan nodded, then gave my shoulder a firm slap. "Godspeed, bro."

"Thanks." I gave him a slap in return and walked to the car, placing our belongings in the trunk.

I walked to the driver's side door and knocked on the window. Ember rolled it down but didn't look at me.

"Do you want me to drive, so you can ... relax?" I'd never been so tongue tied in my life as I was during this situation.

Ember kept looking forward and shook her head. "I need to focus on something else for a while. Let me drive for a few hours."

I walked to the passenger side without a fight, got in, and allowed five full minutes of deafening silence as we navigated toward the highway before I spoke.

"Ember."

"Not right now, Bo. Not ... right now." I watched her cheeks turn crimson as she widened her eyes—her only defense against impending tears.

I ground my back teeth together, impatience and anxiety brewing. Her constant assertion that she could handle things herself was starting to wear on me. All I wanted to do was take care of her. Why was she so resistant?

"We need to talk about what just happened, Ember." My voice was firm but caring as I tried to pry open the gates around her heart.

"You were in the RV with my parents." She shrugged as though that was the answer.

I turned and faced her. "I didn't talk to them about this."

"Why not? They didn't try to cover their asses?" She bit her lip as her tone turned angry.

I reached across the car and set my hand on her leg. She moved it as though she didn't want me to touch her, but I was unfazed. "I'm not in love with them. I wanted to have this conversation with you."

"If I talk about it, I'm going to cry. I hate crying." Her eyes pinched at the edges as early tears seeped out. She was the only person I knew who spent as much time apologizing while she was crying as she did getting to the heart of *why* she was crying.

"Take the next exit." I nodded to the sign that promised good coffee in less than a mile.

"No."

I erased all gentleness from my voice as I battled her stubbornness. "Ember, take the next exit."

She looked at me, most likely checking to see if my face matched my words. When she realized they did, she moved to the right lane and took the exit.

"There's a Starbucks right up there. I know you want one as badly as I do, since the band refuses to let us stop there." I was granted a half smile as Ember negotiated the left hand turn to the church of the mermaid goddess.

Honestly, I wouldn't have cared if it was Starbucks or a gas station, but The Six drank tea and sunshine, leaving little time to stop for the caffeine the rest of us needed. Badly.

"I'll do the drive through, then we can park over there." Ember pointed to the largely vacant lot on the other side of the tiny coffee hut.

I let out a sigh of relief. She was willing to stop the car and drink some coffee. She needed to tell me what happened in that damn RV, and I wasn't letting us back on the highway until I got some answers.

"Yeah," Ember called into the speaker. "I'll have a venti, half-caff, soy, Pike misto with one pump vanilla."

I had to stifle a chuckle. She chanted her order as if it were a daily prayer.

"You want your usual?" She asked me over her shoulder.

"Please."

"And also a venti bold with cream and a shot of boring." She grinned as the barista laughed over the intercom.

Sarcasm was a good sign on Ember's emotional barometer. Even if it was fleeting. Once we retrieved our drinks and paid, she pulled into a parking space and shut the car off after rolling down the windows. I left my coffee in the cup holder, knowing it would be too hot for me to drink for the next several minutes, but I watched Ember take her lid off and close her eyes as she took a deep breath, inhaling the rich aroma of the drink.

After her first sip, she put the lid back on and set the coffee in the holder next to mine. She closed her eyes once more and rested her head against the headrest.

"Well," she sniffed as she let tears roll down her face, "Willow and I really are half sisters."

"Shit," I puffed out my cheeks as I exhaled and grabbed her hand. I knew this information, given Solstice had said it several hours ago, but hearing it from Ember made it more real. "Who ..." I didn't know how to ask which man had fathered two daughters.

"My dad." Her voice went up several octaves as tears choked her tone. "Ashby ... he ... um." Ember leaned forward and pressed her head into the steering wheel.

I unbuckled my seatbelt and leaned over as far as I could, wrapping as much of my body around her as possible, trying to shield her from the internal onslaught of emotions.

She coughed and sniffed as raw tears flooded the inside of our tiny rental car. "He's Willow's biological dad, too."

CHAPTER SIX

NAME

"I knew it," Ember continued as she leaned into my chest but kept her hands on the steering wheel. "I just fucking knew it the second Willow said something to me."

I rested my chin on the top of her head, which was hot from the force of her crying. "Is that why you didn't want to talk to them about it? Your parents, I mean."

I felt her nod beneath my chin. "I knew she had to be right. Why would she make that up?"

"Well ... she's not exactly on high moral ground."

Ember sniffed. "I know. But coming on to you was out of character for her. I knew she was acting out."

"Yeah," I whispered. "I guess."

Finally, Ember sat up, wiped under her eyes, and looked at me. Her eyes weren't as empty as they'd been when she left the RV earlier, but they weren't filled with anything pretty, either. Rage, torment, and a splash of something unidentified. Something I didn't want to try to name.

Ember dug her fingers through her hair and left them resting against her head. "This whole time I was afraid to ask my parents because I didn't want to lose my dad. I knew we didn't share a mom, that much was obvious. So, one of us grew up with the wrong dad. Over the last few months I've looked through all the oldest pictures I could find. I dug through my parents albums, and never once were either Willow or I seen with anyone but our parents in family pictures."

"So what—" I don't know what I started to ask, but Ember cut me off.

"I was so focused on the fear of losing my dad, it never once fucking occurred to me to envision how I'd feel if it was the other way. If he was *also* ... her dad."

I took a sip of my coffee, wishing I'd had something stronger. "Did your mom know? Did ... anyone know but your dad? Did he even know?"

"I don't know how any of us could be surprised, really. For fuck's sake they're all *free love* ..." Ember looked down for a second before turning her gaze out the window.

"*Was* anyone surprised?" I was trying to get details in an order that made sense to me.

"The summer and fall before we were both conceived, they'd just ended a several year run at the top of their charts. They were preparing to take a break then head to the studio for what was slated to be their best album yet. They partied hard, apparently." It seemed as though Ember's tears dried suddenly, and the anger was ready to take center stage.

"November, I'm so sorry. I want to take this away from you, I do." I pulled one of her hands out of her hair and kissed her knuckles, settling our hands on her lap.

"Marry me, then."

"What?" I tilted my head to the side as my ears started to burn.

Ember looked at me with a straight face. "I just told you that my parents never married. That they were part of a culture where that wasn't a requirement. Apparently fidelity wasn't a requirement either, the way it is when people legally marry. I want you to marry me, Bo. I want to be your wife."

"I'm not going to cheat on you, Ember. If you think—"

"This isn't about you!" She slammed her fist on the steering wheel.

"It should be!" I shouted back, startled by her shift in demeanor. "It should be about *us,* Ember, and not you running from your fears or me running from mine. I swear to you, November. I will never, not for a second, break your heart. I've promised you that a million times, and I'll do it a million more. But, what I won't do is marry you because you're scared." She opened her mouth to speak, but I continued, lowering my voice. "When I ask you to marry me, I want you to say yes because you feel like any other answer would be horrifically wrong. I want you to say yes because that's the only rational thing to say. I want you to say yes because you want a life with me. An eternity. I don't want you to say yes because you're scared I'll hurt you if you don't."

I let go of her hand, grabbed my coffee, and opened my door.

"Where are you going?" she snapped.

"Air," I snapped back, slamming the door.

As soon as her door opened, a sinking feeling grew in the pit of my stomach. I never raised my voice to her, and in the span of a few days I'd done it twice. Once because I was afraid, and once because she was. What kind of a husband would that make me?

Ember crossed to my side of the car and held out the keys.

"What's this for?" I asked, barely a grunt coming from my mouth.

"You're driving." She released the keys from her fingers, and I caught them before they tumbled to the ground.

"Fine." I stepped away from the car and got in the driver's side, sliding the seat all the way back and adjusting the mirror as Ember climbed in and buckled her seatbelt.

As I started the car, Ember reached for her cellphone and began texting. That was her signal to me that we were done talking. I wasn't even sure what the hell had just happened between us, but I knew the couple of hours we had left to go till San Francisco were going to be the longest I'd had in a long time.

***

We arrived at Bay Park three hours before our scheduled show. It was enough time to set up the stage, rehearse, and pray like hell we'd be able to pull it off. Truthfully, I wasn't sure there was enough time for that prayer.

Ember and I arrived only a few minutes before The Six caravan did, allowing us to pull our bags from the back of the car and walk to the "shed" that looked like a medium-sized cabin, which sat behind the stage.

When Ember saw the RVs pull in, she walked dutifully to the lead one, which held most of our equipment. And the Shaw family. I watched from a distance as she worked silently to pull mic stands and speakers from below the vehicle and move them to the side of the stage. After a minute, or so, Regan spotted me and jogged over to the shed.

"How was the ride? Is she okay? I texted both of you and no one answered." He fiddled with his hands as he spoke.

"I ended up driving, so I wasn't looking at my phone. She was texting, but if it wasn't to you it must have been to Monica, or someone." I started walking to the second RV, which held the instruments, and he followed.

"So ... what'd she say?" He asked, sounding nervous.

I shrugged. "You were driving with Ash and Raven, did they say anything?"

Regan shook his head. "Silence has never been so loud, dude."

"Tell me about it. All I know is that they're half sisters and," I lowered my voice to a whisper, "Ashby is their biological dad."

"Daaaamn. Is she okay? Ember."

"No. We kind of had a fight during the beginning of the drive. She wasn't really telling me anything that made sense, then she freaked out like I was going to cheat on her, or something. We'll talk about it more later, okay?" I nodded behind Regan, where I saw the rest of the band approaching. Including Willow.

While the band shifted awkwardly around each other, I made eye contact with Ashby, silently begging him for guidance in this situation. He seemed to understand, and nodded toward the shed, asking me to follow him. Ember had her head down as she worked to unravel cord and do sound checks, so she didn't seem to notice my departure.

I shut the door to the shed behind me while Ashby paced the floor for a moment. Finally, he sat in a chair against the wall, motioning for me to take the one next to him.

"How is she?" He spoke with the same heartbreaking vulnerability Ember did. The similarities between the two made this even harder somehow.

I sighed as I sat, rubbing my forehead with my sweaty palm. "Jesus, Ash ... not good. Can you tell me what the hell happened?"

"She didn't tell you?"

"It came out in pieces. You're Willow's biological father. You and Raven aren't married. Apparently those two go together equal Ember's assertion that we have to get married immediately." I looked to Ashby, who frowned as he sat back.

"We just weren't careful, Bo. It's not like we were swingers, in the traditional sense, but the four of us—me and Raven, and Solstice and Michael—had a very open relationship for years. *Years.* This conversation could just as easily be happening the other way, with Michael at the helm."

I scoffed. It was meant to be silent. It wasn't, and I could tell it hurt Ashby's feelings.

"You can't judge us, Bo. It was a lifestyle we all chose. We never meant for anyone to get hurt."

I stood, pacing the short length of the room with my hands in my back pockets. "Someone did get hurt, though. Two someones, and it was none of the four of you who made that original decision, Ash. Those girls didn't get to decide this. Now Ember is in full panic mode, and I don't know how to help her. She's pulling away, though I'm sure me losing my temper didn't help. Why didn't you guys tell them when they were growing up? Did all four of you know?"

Ashby nodded. "We all knew, but not until the girls were two. That's when Michael found out he couldn't have children. He and

Solstice had been trying for a sibling for Willow, and it wasn't working. They went to a doctor, and …"

"So Willow could be anyone's child, then?" I stopped and turned on my heels to face him again.

He shook his head. "It was just the four of us, no one else. We were monogamous in our group … if that makes sense." He looked up at me with the shame of a two and a half decade-old decision scrolling over his face.

"None of this makes sense. Why didn't you tell them?"

Ashby sighed and stood. "By the time we found out, we'd all bonded in our families. I didn't feel closer to Willow just by learning she was biologically mine. And, Michael didn't feel any distance from her. We accepted the results of our actions and agreed to just … keep our families the way they were. It would have been too confusing otherwise. We did what we thought was right, I—"

I cut him off as he started to ramble through his guilt. "I really don't mean to judge, Ashby. I'm just trying to understand how I can help Ember. How's Willow, anyway?"

"Same. Though it seems that she was resolved this would be the outcome, so it didn't come down on her as hard as it came down on Ember. I'm scared I lost my little girl, Bo. I've spent twenty-eight years falling in love with her, and the way she looked at me today … it was like she was staring at a stranger." Ashby put his hand over his mouth as a sob escaped.

"Christ." I walked over to him and pulled him into a hug. If nothing else, spending all of this time with Raven and Ashby taught me how to love them. Ashby needed a hug.

After a long five seconds, Ashby cleared his throat and pulled away. "Do you think she'll be okay to do the show tonight?"

"If for no other reason than to spite all of us, yes." I smirked, and he followed. "Is Willow going to stay on tour with us?" I'm not sure what answer I'd hoped for.

Ashby nodded, and I realized I'd been hoping for the opposite movement. "She will. We asked both girls to stay. We don't want or expect them to suddenly behave like the family they are, but we can't bear to have them at each other's throats anymore."

"Ash?" Raven knocked on the door to the shed. "We're ready to do sound checks. Are you guys all right?"

Ashby looked at me hopefully, and I nodded. He called over my shoulder. "We'll be right out, hun." He redirect his words to me. "Let's get through the shows tonight and tomorrow. Then we have a couple of days before the next one to hopefully sort through some things."

I opened the door, motioning for Ashby to exit ahead of me. "Here goes nothing, huh?"

CHAPTER SEVEN

SING, SING, SING

THANKFULLY, I WAS right about Ember's ability to keep her stage life and off-stage life separate for the sake of the show. It was something I'd always been able to do. I found performing the best way to work through whatever was happening off stage. Luckily for all of us, and the audience, Ember and the rest of The Six did the same.

The last song before intermission had me nervous, and holding my breath. While the whole band was involved instrumentally, the vocal showcase belonged to Ember and her mom, while Ashby and I led the melody on our guitars.

Ember looked as poised as ever as she stood inches away from her mother, sharing a microphone as they sang:

Sing, baby, sing, baby, sing tonight
Sing for the good and sing for the bad,
oh sing for the life you thought you had

I took an anxious breath but Ember kept smiling. It may have been my imagination, but her vocals sounded better than they had in a long time.

Kiss me sweetly, one last time
Kiss me like we never lost our shine
Hold on tight, and tighter still
Breathe in the life we had together
The life we never will

Oh,
Sing, baby, sing, baby, sing tonight
Hold me, kiss me, love me
Through the night
Sunrise comes, shadows disappear
The only thing we're left with, baby
Is our fear

I exhaled loudly as Ashby and I strummed the lengthy interlude, before the gorgeous mother-daughter team finished out the last song of this set.

Oh, fear is a hearty mistress, cutting no slack
Grab my hand, stop looking back
The moonlight is ours, the sunlight for us.
Baby, nothing comes between us
No matter the cost.

Once the song ended, and the crowd lifted us up with their applause, we announced our short break and headed to the shed.

"That was stunning, Ember." I tugged her hand until her body was against mine, kissing her neck as I spoke.

She overrode my system every time she sang. I'd fallen in love with her on a stage, and every time we took one together. It felt like that first night all over again, only it was better. Now she was mine.

Ember squeezed my hand and backed away from my lips. "Come with me."

She pulled me through the back door, where we were greeted by a large field and the canopy of every star in the universe hovering over us. The crowd hummed on the other side of the sage, but they seemed a million miles away as Ember led me down a small hill, sitting us in tall grass dotted with wildflowers.

I sat next to her and wrapped my arm around her shoulders, pulling her flush with me once again.

She lifted her face to me, allowing me to kiss her nose, making her smile as she spoke. "I'm sorry for this morning."

I took my other arm and squeezed her tighter. "I'm the one who's sorry. You have nothing to be sorry for. I was an asshole for losing my temper with you."

Ember sat back, crossing her legs as she grabbed my hands, the intensity of her gaze grounding me. "No. I'm sorry for not telling you everything. You deserve more than my tantrum, Bo. We're a fucking team. You remember that. Every day you tell me what you're feeling, good and bad. No matter how much it hurts. You let me ask you about nightmares you have in the middle of the night, and you answer me even if its two thirty in the morning. You would never dream of brushing me off like I did to you today."

"Ember, I've had years of therapy that's allowed me to do that. It's hard, but it's the only way I can ever keep myself from shutting down completely." I brushed a loose wave of hair away from her eyes, tucking it behind her ear.

She twisted her lips in apparent embarrassment. "I'm sorry for asking you to marry me."

I laughed once, loudly. "You're forgiven. Try not to let it happen again, K?"

"What?" she teased. "I can't ask you to marry me? Women can propose, you know."

I twiched my mouth into a grin. "Not to me, they can't."

"Are you some sort of a caveman?"

"I am." I nodded definitively.

"Hmm, I'll take it." She turned her back, settling herself between my knees and leaning her head against my chest. "Seriously, though. I should have told you everything. In order. I'm not mad at you. I'm just ... heartbroken." Her voice cut off at the end of her sentence, and the tightening of her shoulders cued me into the tears that were undoubtedly rolling down her face.

I swept her hair over one shoulder, allowing me access to her tear-soaked cheeks, where I kissed some of them away. "It's okay to be hurting. Your dad kind of filled me in when we got here. Not the gory details, but about their ... open relationship with Michael and Solstice." I held my breath, unsure if my words would push her too hard.

"I don't even know what I'm most upset about. Not knowing I had a sister this whole time, or that I have one at all."

"Well," I offered, "you and Willow were close when you were younger, right?"

She nodded. "We were. And last year, when you and I got here, Willow and I were as close as we'd always been. It hurt like hell when she came on to you, Bo. It came out of nowhere. She had a reputation, but it had never affected me or my relationship with her. We were like sisters. Turns out, we are *actually* sisters, and she was taking it out on me."

"Did she know your dad was also her dad?"

"I think she knew. It's pretty fucking obvious now, isn't it? It's like she was punishing me for being the one who got to *keep* my dad, or something. Even though it feels like the exact opposite ..." She trailed off and took a deep breath, exhaling as her shoulders sank.

"You feel like you lost him?"

"I feel like I don't know him at all, Bo. I mean, sure, I knew that he and my mom weren't married. But, I thought they were one of those special couples that stayed together because they chose each other, over and over again every day because they wanted to and not because there were legal documents that demanded their togetherness."

"Your dad said—"

Ember sat forward and put her hand up, waving it around. "I'm not ready for what he said, okay? I just need to talk about how I'm feeling. My gut reactions." She turned and looked at me with a determination I was glad to see.

I nodded, smiling that she and I appeared to be on even ground again. "Talk away, love. I'll listen to every word you say."

Ember turned and smiled. "I like that you call me *love*. Do that always."

"Always," I whispered.

She leaned forward, pressing my back against the grass as she kissed the hell out of me. I moaned louder than I'd intended to, given we weren't exactly anywhere private, but it felt so good to be home on her lips again. I hadn't kissed her since we woke up, and that was far too damn long to have my mouth away from hers.

She pulled away with a smug grin on her face. "Get your act together, rockstar. We have another set. First act is me, you, and Regan."

I groaned, playfully biting her shoulder as I sat up. "You expect me to be alone on stage with you with *that* kiss in my head?"

"Think of it as motivation. For tonight."

"Tonight?" I stood and held out my hand, helping her to her feet.

"We're getting a hotel room. You think I'm going to sleep in an RV with either my parents *or* Willow?"

I placed my hands on her backside, pulling her close to my body. "Not if we're going to do what I plan to do with you." I whispered into her ear, grinning as I felt goosebumps against my lips.

"Bo Cavanaugh," she whispered back, "are you teasing me?"

I bit my lip, tilting my head to the side. "No. Promising."

"Guys!" A slightly frantic sounding Regan hollered out the back door. "Let's gooooo!"

"Tonight," I promised, grinning at her before acknowledging Regan.

"Tonight."

Regan introduced us, and we took our stools, Ember and I slinging our guitars over our shoulders as we smiled to one another. Whistles and claps came from the crowd.

"Kiss her!" someone shouted from the front row.

Without hesitation, I flicked on my mic and answered, "You don't have to ask me twice."

Reaching out my hand, I slipped it around the back of Ember's neck and pulled her to me, the crowd growing louder in their hoots and hollers.

Ember bit her lip and arched her eyebrow as she pulled away. "Ready?"

I answered with the strum of my guitar, and she fell into step a measure later. Performing looked good on her. Her cheeks glowed, her eyes brightened, and even her hair seemed to bounce more as she shook her head with the beat. She was surrendering herself to the music, and it was even a sexier sight than when she was under me in our bed.

Just as I thought that was an exaggeration—because when she was naked I could barely separate reason from fantasy—she opened her mouth and reminded me of the exact moment I fell in love with her. When I first heard her voice.

Lost ... and found
We're taking the long way,
Oh, the long way around ...

She was singing a song that she, Regan and I had reworked from The Six's first album. As with most of their early work, there was a lot of male/female back and forth. I had to keep count as I played, because getting lost in her voice was as easy as falling in love with her had been and I constantly risked missing my entrance. I hoped that would never go away.

Lifting my eyes from her mouth up to Regan, who helped count me in, I saw a tender smile on his face. I knew how much he missed having Georgia around, especially since they were fairly early in their relationship, but his undying support for my relationship with Ember was reassuring. He was the best friend I'd had in many years.

On his nod, I entered the song, silently grateful he was diligent in counting. The feeling I had when my voice joined Ember's surged through my body like electricity, causing me to smile as we sang. As our melodies joined in holy matrimony I longed for our souls to.

Watching her head lower as she worked over a difficult combination on her guitar, and nailing it, I was once again firm in my resolve that she would be my wife. And I would spend the rest of my life working my ass off to be the husband she deserved.

***

"I hope Regan doesn't hate us for bailing on him." I discarded my backpack on the floor next to our bed in the small inn a few miles from the concert site.

Ember slid her sandals under the desk and slowly lifted her shirt. "Are we really going to talk about Regan? He's a big boy. He'll be fine."

"Regan who?" I ran my tongue across my bottom lip as I walked toward Ember, stopping her hands as they reached the waistband of her skirt.

"Are you stopping me from being without clothes? That seems … counterproductive."

She followed my eyes and let out a small groan as I knelt down in front of her, and she ran her slender fingers through my hair. Once I was on my knees, I guided the navy floor-length skirt over her hips, slowly brushing my fingers along the curve of her outer thigh and over the slight muscle in her calf.

"How is your skin always this soft?" I whispered as I brought my lips to her knee, trailing kisses down to her ankle where I let the skirt crumple to the floor.

Ember stepped backward and away from the skirt, standing before me in nothing but flushed cheeks and a nude lace thong. Her hair fell to just below her breasts, and she stood still, never breaking my stare.

Sitting back on my heels, I spoke again. "You're the most beautiful thing I've ever seen." My breath was fast and shallow as all of my clothes suddenly seemed ill-fitting.

Taking two steps forward, Ember held her hand out to me. As I stood, she spoke in the husky whisper I'd come to associate with the warmth of my tongue against her skin. "I need you, Bo. Make love to me."

I lowered my head as she lifted slightly on her toes, clutching the fabric of my shirt as she pressed her swollen lips into mine. She lifted my shirt over my head, returning her lips to my collarbone, and worked her way slowly across my chest.

Unbuttoning my shorts as quickly as I could, I cast them to the floor along with my boxer briefs.

"Now *you* have too much clothing on," I murmured against her skin as I ran my thumb along the elastic of her thong.

Like a dance, Ember took one step back toward the bed and I answered with one step forward. As she sat, I pulled her thong the rest of the way off. She responded by tossing her hair back over her shoulders, allowing me full access to her hardened nipples.

"Kiss me. Here." She skimmed her fingers across her breasts as she scooted up the bed, laying back and pulling me on top of her.

I started at her neck, enjoying the restless squirming of her hips as my lips journeyed to their destination. As my tongue encircled the first nipple, Ember cried out and arched her back.

"God, Bo ... I need you inside me." She pressed the pads of her fingers into my shoulders, highlighting her urgency.

As I ran a hand up her inner thigh, connecting with the warm center of her desire, I felt the intensity of her need and couldn't even pretend to hold back. Pushing her knees far enough apart to let me square myself between them, I paused for a moment, hovering over her as her hips continued their desperate movements.

Arresting her eyes in my gaze, I spoke softly but firmly. "November ... I will never *ever* hurt you."

Tears streamed from the corners of her eyes as she grabbed my hips and led me into her, throwing her head back as I filled her. As her tight space squeezed around me before relaxing and allowing me full access, I gritted my teeth, losing myself in the feeling.

I pulled out slowly and immediately pushed in. Harder this time. Needing to feel the pressure of her body around me.

"Shit," I hissed as Ember drew her knees back, letting me fall deeper into her as she gripped the backs of my legs.

"Go slow. Just for a minute." Her eyes opened and locked with mine, and I couldn't look away. I couldn't close my eyes.

I slowed down, pulling out slowly once more, and entering her just as slow, watching her eyes widen just slightly each time I entered her.

My heart raced and I felt lightheaded. "I can't go slow anymore," I pleaded.

"What do you want?" she whispered, running her hand along the outside of my face.

"I want to make you come." I tried to slow my breathing by inhaling through my nose, trying not to lose it in that moment.

Ember lifted her head, setting her lips just to the side of my ear, and whispered, "Take what you want."

As her head fell back to the pillow, I clenched my hands around the sheets and worked faster and harder, moaning as she screamed my name.

"God, Ember ... I can't hold on much longer." My voice was a barely recognizable growl.

She cried out again as she released her hands from my back and found my hands on the bed, locking her fingers with mine. "Come with me, Bo. Now."

The second I felt the swell of her orgasm crash around me, I let go. Pulsing deeply as we both called to each other from the depths of our ecstasy. Once our breathing slowed, I grabbed her chin, moving her face so she'd look at me.

"Never," I repeated my promise from earlier. "Do you hear me? I'm never, *ever* going to make you feel one ounce of sorrow."

With a quivering chin, Ember nodded, tears rising through her tired green eyes. "I trust you."

Slowly I slid out of her, rolling to my side and pulling her still-warm body against my chest. Nuzzling through her hair, my lips found her neck. She responded by pressing her back even tighter against my body.

"Bo?" she asked in the smallest voice I'd heard from her in a long time.

"Yes, love?"

"Hold me until I fall asleep."

I sighed, wanting more than anything to take away the raw pain that sat in her heart. "I'll hold you *while* you sleep. Always."

I kissed her temple once, and rested my head against the pillow, listening to the lush sound of her breath slow and even out until she was asleep. Planting my lips on her shoulder, I allowed sleep to take me, too. Praying that when we woke, her pain would miraculously be gone.

CHAPTER EIGHT

THE MEDIATOR

NO MIRACLES WERE granted the next morning. While Ember's nerves no longer seemed exposed, the pain was still there. Forced under the surface of her manufactured smile as we ate breakfast with the band and prepared for the afternoon show. No one tried to talk to her about anything other than the music, and, for those few hours, I was grateful.

The show went even better than the previous night. Ember's ability to compartmentalize served the group's interests, but had me concerned for her. I could barely look at her dad, because the pained expression in his eyes as he watched the daughter he raised was nearly enough to bring me to my knees.

The band worked quickly to pack the RVs after the second show, and the awkward silence was broken by something unbelievably more awkward. As Ember closed one of the doors beneath one RV, Willow came around the back side, putting the resistant sisters face to face.

Willow looked as though she was going to turn and go around the other side, but Ember spoke, reaching her hand out and touching Willow's arm.

"Can we talk?" Ember tilted her head to the empty RV. I felt the breath of every member of the band come to a halt behind me.

Willow looked down, and the color in her cheeks deepen as she looked up again. "Yeah," she whispered and wove through those of us who were frozen in our places, entering the RV without another word.

Ember turned slowly, looking at only me. She tugged on my fingertips and gave me a quick peck on the cheek. Putting her head down and ignoring everyone else, she followed Willow into the vehicle and shut the door.

"Well," Regan piped up, clapping his hands once, "this is awkward."

A mix of nervous laughter and uncomfortable grumbles rose through the group.

"We'll be in the other RV," Mags announced, speaking for herself and Journey. "Regan, do you want to join us?"

"Sure, why the hell not?" He shrugged and gave a bright and nervous smile as he passed by me. "We're painting *The Mediator* on the side of that RV."

I grinned as I shook my head. "If they both come out alive, you've got yourself a deal."

Once the uninvolved trio disappeared into the second vehicle, four sets of eyes turned on me.

"What?" I asked, widening my eyes.

Ashby spoke first. "How'd you get Ember to ... talk to Willow."

"Ash, we both know no one can make Ember do a goddam thing. We didn't talk much last night after the show. We just kind of passed out." Warmth ran through my veins at the memory of what we had *actually* done.

Raven wrapped her hand around my forearm. "That may be so, but your influence on our daughter can't go unnoticed. You ground her. And she does the same for you. You're each others' emotional center." She spoke softly, arresting me with her hopeful eyes.

For the first time in twenty-four hours, I heard Michael speak as he wrapped his arm around his wife's waist. "We're sorry it blew up like this."

I shrugged. "I can't imagine how it felt to face those choices. I really can't. I don't know what I would have done, but I know you did what you thought was the right thing."

Solstice rested her head on her husband's shoulder, looking longingly at the dark RV. "Hopefully those two feel the same way. They're just so … angry."

"Is Willow angry with you two?" I asked, hoping for help on how to comfort Ember. Somehow.

Michael's eyes misted over. "She was at first. Of course she's been grappling with this for who knows how long, even though it was unconfirmed. Then, she came to me in the middle of the night last night, crying. She thanked me for loving her like she was my own. I told her she *was* mine …" He trailed off, looking somewhere in the distance.

"Ember hasn't spoken to either of us," Ashby offered up, sitting on a bench behind him and placing his head in his hands.

"Sometimes," I started, cutting off Raven who looked like she was about to speak, "it's best to give her a little space. I kind of speak from experience there." I sat next to Ashby, patting his back once.

He stared blankly at the ground. "She looked at me like I was a filthy miscreant. I never imagined a look like that coming from my baby girl. I love her ... just so damn much ..."

Solstice and Michael moved next to Ashby, and Raven squatted in front of him. The four of them weren't behaving any differently with each other. They were best friends, and, apparently, they were seeing this through together.

"If you guys don't mind, I'm going to take a walk." I rose and headed through the parking lot to the field where Ember and I sat last night before the show.

Just as I settled into the grass, my phone rang. It was Monica.

"Hey, Mon."

"Holy shitballs, Cavanaugh, what the *hell* is going on in the Redwood Forest?" Her panic didn't affect me because my anxiety was three steps above hers.

"We're not in the Redwood's, Monica." I tried to use humor to calm her down.

"Shut up."

It didn't work.

"When did you talk to Ember? What'd she tell you?" I wasn't about to tell a story Ember wanted to tell herself.

"That trampy willow branch is her fucking sister?! Now Ember isn't answering her phone, and I don't—"

"Mon, Mon ... Mon," I repeated her name until she calmed down. "Ember and Willow are talking right now and, no, I don't know what about."

Monica growled into the phone. I could picture the hot-headed trucker-mouthed brunette getting herself into a tizzy. "Ember calls me at *three in the morning* and sobs the whole story, then tells me *not to worry* about it and she'll see me in two *fucking* weeks?"

I bit the inside of my cheek, upset that in my exhaustion I didn't realize my girlfriend had left the bed and was falling apart in a bathroom ten feet away.

"What do you want me to say, Monica?"

Her tone turned deadly serious. "Say you're not going to bail."

"What?" I looked up to the sky, silently begging God for a Monica Decoder Ring.

"Ember told me about your pleasant little panic attack a few days ago where you asked her to marry you in your living room. She told me, also, about her meltdown in the Starbucks parking lot. She's afraid that those conversations, mixed with what's going on in her family, will cause you to pull away."

Monica's words hit me in the center of the chest. Ember and I had just spent a beautiful night together, where I promised her that those exact things *wouldn't* happen. Still, she woke hysterical in the middle of the night and poured it all out to her best friend who was more than three thousand miles away.

"Bo," Monica quipped. "You're not going to fucking run, are you?"

I stood up and snapped, "No! I love her. Forever. What the hell is with you two? Why can't you accept that. I love her. I'm in love with her and only her and I want to marry her. You know that, Mon. I was going to do it when you were here in two weeks. Now, with all this stuff with her dad, I just … I don't know if that'll happen."

"What, the proposal?"

"No, just not then. If she's not on good terms with her family, there's no way I can ask her. It doesn't feel right."

"Do you have the ring?" Monica asked, shifting direction.

"What?"

"Ring. Do you have one?"

I cleared my throat. "I've had it for a long time. It's my moms. I had the stones re-set into a ring that's much more Ember-like."

"When did you have it re-set?"

"I'm not telling you." I chuckled. "You'll think I'm ridiculous."

Monica clicked her tongue. "I already think you two are far beyond ridiculous. When did you have it re-set?"

"The day after your wedding," I mumbled.

"Hot damn! Bo Cavanaugh, I'll be out there the day after tomorrow. This nuclear meltdown is the job of a best friend. Sit tight, don't tell her I'm coming, then we can get about the business."

I grinned at her demands. "The business of what?"

"Marrying Ember."

All the air left my lungs, and apparently, Monica heard.

"Bo? You alive over there?"

"You're absolutely right, Monica."

"Of course, but about what?"

"I'm going to marry Ember." I began pacing an erratic path through the grass.

"No shit, Bo. That's what all of this is—"

"No. Listen. You were coming out here for me to propose to Ember, right?"

"Yeeeessss," Monica drew out cautiously.

"Screw all of that. I'm just going to get down to it."

Monica huffed frustratedly. "Down to what?"

I smiled as broadly as I had in days. "Marrying Ember. I'm going to *marry her*, Monica." A million lightbulbs flashed through my body. "It's me. It's her. I'm going to marry her. Just ... marry her."

After a long silence, Monica finally spoke. "All men should just go ahead and give up now. You're not even real. Seriously. Do *noth-*

ing except plan. I will be there the day *after* tomorrow. If I show up and you're married ... I'll cut you."

I laughed. "I know you will. And, I won't be. I need to get her and her dad back on speaking terms. And, you have to help."

"On it. Bye."

"Bye."

I slid my phone into my pocket and walked back to the parking lot just in time to see Ember handing Willow the keys to our rental car. I jogged over to the pair, noting that their parents were all still where I'd left them. Ember had our guitars and backpacks resting on the edge of the parking lot, leaving me to assume our time with the tiny rental car was over.

"What's, uh, going on?" The adrenaline my body produced while talking with Monica made me sound more out of breath than I actually was.

Willow gave a weak smile and looked to Ember, who spoke. "Willow's going to take the car and head back to San Diego."

As I studied their faces, I didn't see any signs of distress.

"I'm ... confused," I admitted.

"Bo," Willow started, seemingly unable to meet my eyes. "I just want to tell you how sorry I am for the way I've behaved. Honestly, I'm embarrassed. Before all of this, Ember was my best childhood friend ... I didn't mean ..."

"Hey," I walked over to her and gave her a firm, but friendly, hug, "it's okay. Everyone reacts differently to stress." I had a lot more I wanted to say to her, but it seemed that only pure kindness was called for in that minute.

Willow pulled back and wiped under her eyes. "Anyway, I'm going to go back home and kind of chill out for a while. I'll fly back up at the end of next week for the Napa show. Until then, I just want the dust to settle. And, since I'm not actually in the band, it makes the most sense for me to leave."

Ember tugged gently on one of Willow's mile-long braids. "You know you don't *have* to go, though."

Willow turned to her. "I know. But I also know it will be a lot harder for you to work things out with your dad with me hanging around."

"I don't know what I have to say to him." Ember crossed her arms in front of her body.

"And it will be a lot harder to figure out if I'm looming in the background."

"How are you not furious?" Ember asked, leaving me happy she was openly conversing with Willow in front of me.

Willow hooked her thumb in my direction. "I *was* furious, remember? I was mad that you got to keep your dad ... that you got to have the true, perfect and real family. And the perfect boyfriend. I wanted to take something from you. Like I felt something had been taken from me."

I winced at the honesty in her words, but Ember didn't flinch.

"You have your dad, Willow."

"Right," Willow answered, rubbing Ember's arms, "and you have yours."

As Ember nodded, Willow pulled her into a hug. I looked passed them, to the girls' parents, and saw them openly staring, and intermittently wiping under their eyes.

"Drive safe," Ember said as she backed up, allowing Willow to open the driver's door.

"I will. See you in ten days." Willow smiled as she turned the key.

"See you." Ember shut the door and Willow pulled away.

I put my arm around her and she rested her head on my shoulder. "Where's our next gig?" she asked tiredly.

I looked up for a moment, scanning the schedule that I had stored in my brain. "Vallejo this weekend, then we go straight to Napa and spend a few days there before our show at the end of next week."

"Okay," she murmured.

"So ... I hesitate to ask this, but ... which RV are we going to ride in now? I'm only asking because we have reservations at a park in Vallejo tonight and the office there closes in an hour and a half." It was only a forty-minute drive, but given the way this road trip had gone, we needed a broad margin of error.

"Same as before. I'll just ... need some space from my parents."

"In an RV? Not a problem ..." I turned her around so she was facing me, and I stroked my thumbs down the sides of her face.

She quirked her mouth into a sarcastic grin. "You know what I mean."

I hugged her, resting my chin on the top of her head. "Yeah, beautiful, I know. You know what else I know?"

"What's that?" she looked up at me through her feathery lashes.

"I know that your dad would do anything for you. He's felt as helpless as I have, Ember. He wants to take this pain away but there is *nothing* he can do. And, it's killing him."

Ember's eyes filled with huge tears, and in the span of a blink they were released down her face. "This is so screwed up." She pressed her forehead into my chest and her shoulders shook.

"I know, love. I know." I rubbed her back, setting my chin on her head once more.

I watched as Solstice and Michael got in their RV, and Regan walked toward us with his hands in his pockets. I knew it had been difficult for him to see Ember going through this and feeling like he didn't have anything useful to say. As he approached us, Raven and Ashby slowly entered our RV, Ashby shooting a glance over his shoulder just before he climbed the stairs.

"Em ..." Regan put a hand on her back and looked to me. I mouthed *she's okay*, just as Ember straightened up and faced him.

"Hey you. Sorry for blowing you off yesterday." She wrapped her arms around his neck and he squeezed her into a tight hug.

"No sorry's, remember? I know you needed a minute." Regan and Ember were constantly teasing each other for apologizing for how they were feeling.

Ember started for our things at the edge of the lot. "Is my dad driving tonight?" she called over her shoulder.

"Yeah. It's a short drive though," I assured her.

Ember picked up her guitar case and hooked her messenger bag on her shoulder. "Regan, I'll fill you in once we get settled at the park and can get away for a while, okay?"

"Sure thing."

With baited breath, I entered the RV after Regan and Ember. Ashby started the vehicle as I ascended the stairs. His eyes flicked to mine for a second. I attempted a reassuring smile, placing a firm hand on his shoulder as I walked by him and to the back of the RV. Ember and Regan had taken their seats at the table we'd sat when this journey began. Raven was in the middle, perched in a lotus position on a cushion, meditation music blaring from her earbuds. The irony made me chuckle.

Regan put his earbuds in and rested his head against the window, and Ember sat next to him, plugging hers in as well, and closed her eyes. For a few minutes as we rolled up the highway, I watched the colors of the sunset paint their way over her face and hair.

I took a deep breath, trying to ground myself as I felt the weight of my changed plans. A hard lump of hopefulness formed in my throat as I watched her head tilt to the side as sleep overtook her. Her cheek landed on Regan's shoulder, who looked startled for a moment before looking at me curiously.

"What's going on?" he whispered as quietly as he could.

"I'm gonna marry her," I whispered back, even quieter.

Regan smiled, looking down at his sleeping friend—the love of my life—before glancing back at me. "Perfect."

CHAPTER NINE

MOVING PIECES

THE AMOUNT OF downtime that faced us filled me with anxiety. We had two days until the Vallejo show, and a whole week after that before the next set of shows in Napa.

The night we got to Vallejo, Ember, as promised, caught Regan up on everything. The following day, everyone kind of went their own ways, rambling around Vallejo for the day. Ember skillfully avoided both her parents, and any conversation about them.

"You've been weird today. Is everything okay?" Ember asked as we wound through the end of a trail at the edge of the park where we were staying.

There was a large rock to my left. I stopped at it, pulling Ember with me and making her sit. I was on edge about Monica's arrival, hoping she'd get here with words of wisdom, but in the meantime, I had to try.

"What's going on?" Ember asked.

"I need you to hear me here, okay?"

She shrugged. "Sure."

"You know I wouldn't say this if I didn't fully mean it with everything I have. I don't use it as a social crutch …"

"What are you talking about?"

"Ember … you have both of your parents. And you get to spend every day with them doing exactly what you all love doing—"

"Stop." Ember stood and started walking toward the head of the trail. "You don't get to make me feel guilty. I'm sorry my parents are still alive, but that doesn't mean I never get to be mad at them."

"*You* stop." I caught up to her and grabbed her upper arm, spinning her around. Her lips parted, seeming breathless at the forcefulness in my voice. "Listen. You *know* I don't mean it as a guilt trip. We've been over this for almost a year. Just because it now applies to you doesn't mean you get to go back on your word, Ember. I'm trying to tell you how much your dad loves you. He's the only man in the universe who loves you more than I could ever dream of. And that's a fact."

"Why are you pushing me?" She closed her mouth and clenched her teeth.

"Pushing you? I haven't said a *thing*. You asked me to run interference with them, and for the last two days I've done just that. It's time to move, Ember. It's time to face it."

In a second, her facade deflated like a balloon. Her shoulders sank and her face paled. "What if I can't?" she whispered, looking up at me through wide eyes.

I lifted her chin with my index finger. "You can. I'll be there with you if you need me to be. Or I'll wait in the woods if that's what you want. Every day of your life, Ember, I'll be there when you need me. And, when you think you don't, I'll still be there. Just in case."

She shifted her lips, kissing my finger. "I need you every day."

"Let's go, then." I nodded to the trailhead, where I knew the group was likely returning to the campsite.

As we reached the edge of the trail, a shrill sound that could only be described as *girl* pierced my ears.

"Ember!" As Ember and I made our way to the clearing, Monica sped at lightning speed toward us, nearly tackling Ember to the ground with her hug.

"Monca?! You're not supposed to be here for another week!" Ember shrieked and the friends jumped up and down.

"Just a *hi* will do." Walking toward us, next to Regan, Georgia spoke dryly, with a smirk.

"Georgia? What the hell?" Ember ignored Georgia's request, and gave her a hug as well. One that Georgia graciously returned.

"Well, I hired someone to help my mom with the bakery because I was tired of missing all the fun. Monica called me and told me about her travel plans, so I jumped on board."

Ember looked between Monica and Georgia. "You guys haven't met before."

Monica rolled her eyes. "Jesus, Ember, do you think I'd trust my best friend around any old female? Hell no. I got to the bottom of that shit, and quick. Georgia and I have been chatting for a while ..."

As the girls walked toward the lake in a cackle of giggles and erratic hand motions, Monica looked over her shoulder and gave me a wink. When they disappeared out of sight, I turned to Regan, who looked as shellshocked as I felt.

"What was that?" I asked.

"This is what I gathered when I picked them up from the airport." He took a comically deep breath while he looked to the sky. "Apparently, once you talked to Monica about discussing the engagement with Georgia, Monica looked up the bakery phone number and gave Georgia a thorough interrogation regarding her friendship credentials."

I scrunched my nose. "How'd Georgia handle that one?"

"Well, apparently she told Monica to back the fuck off, and Monica told her that she passed the test. They both laughed, and that was that."

"Okay," I sat down at the nearest picnic table, "that doesn't explain how they both ended up here at the same time."

Regan sat next to me. "Oh, right. Well, once I got the story on everything the other day with Ember, I called Georgia. She's my girlfriend, I get to tell her stuff."

"Of course."

"Apparently, then, Georgia called Monica to make sure she knew what was going on, because they both know that Ember can be oddly reserved. Even with people she loves."

I nodded in approval. "Score one for Georgia."

"Right? Anyway, I guess since Monica had already talked to you and Ember, they knew what was going on …" Regan looked up reluctantly.

"What …"

"See … Monica told Georgia that she thinks you're going to marry Ember like asap. Maybe even before Napa. And I couldn't deny it, even though I don't know what the hell is going on ever, so Georgia told me she wasn't missing any of this for the world, the girls arranged their flights and … well … here we are." He gave an overstated, toothy smile at the end of his sentence.

I leaned forward and put my head in my hands. "Can Georgia keep a secret?" I realized how ridiculous the question was right when it came out of my mouth.

"Dude ..."

"Dumb question, I know ... None of this is going to happen until I can: A. Get Ember on speaking terms with her dad again, B. I ask him for permission to marry her. According to Monica I can't do till right before because *he* can't keep a secret. Which, by the way is the most ironic statement of the year, and C. Ember has to say yes and go through with it." I wiped my hands over my shorts a million times, but couldn't dry them as panic rose.

"Let's, uh, slow it down ... shall we?" Regan left the table and ran into one of the RVs, returning with two miraculously chilled bottles of beer.

I took a few large gulps and sighed my relief. "Thanks, man. Sorry."

"We know she's going to say yes. We know her dad is going to say yes. One of them is ordained, right?"

"One of who?"

"The Six. Isn't Journey ordained?"

I pulled my eyebrows in. "How the *hell* do you know that?"

"I was trapped in an RV with them the other day, remember? I know more than I'll ever repeat, dude." He lifted his eyes to the sky and shook his head with a comical grin on his face.

"The only problem with involving her is it's one more person who needs to keep it a secret—" I cut myself off and stood, slapping Regan upside his head.

Regan ducked back and put his hand to his head. "What the hell, bro?"

"I've got it!" My heart raced as I formed the plan in my head. "Tonight. It's happening tonight. Text Georgia, tell her to keep them all away until its dark. Like ... stars out, dark."

Regan pulled his cell from his pocket and typed out a quick text. "Done."

As if I needed more proof that what I was doing was right in the perfect time, Journey, and the rest of The Six returned from their hike.

"Bo? What's up? You look ... hyper." Raven studied me curiously.

I took a deep breath, looked to Regan who gave me a thumbs up, then I addressed the group.

"Journey, we need to talk. Walk with me?"

CHAPTER TEN

COMING HOME

Ember

"Guys, come on, we've been out all day. Can we *please* go back now." After a full afternoon in the sun with Georgia and Monica, including drinks on the pier, I was exhausted.

"I guess, but I've never been here before. Cut me some slack." Monica looped her arm through mine as we made our way through the streets heading back to the campground.

Georgia was on my other side, and I linked arms with her, too. She shot me a surprised look, then took a step closer to me as we continued our walk.

When Georgia spoke, her voice was softer around the edges than I was used to. "Thanks for including me."

I nudged her with my shoulder. "Of course. You've been a huge part of my life for the last several months, and you make one my best friends wicked happy—"

"I know," she smiled, "but I've also never had close girlfriends before. And we didn't really get off to the best start."

"The good news is, it doesn't end where you start, unless you quit. We didn't quit each other."

Monica stopped in her tracks and tugged my wrist.

"What?" I asked, studying her serious expression.

"Unless you quit ..."

"Yeah?" I drew out, looking around.

Monica shot a look to Georgia before addressing me. "Look, Em ... I wasn't going to bring this up right now, but ..." She looked down, biting her lip in an uncharacteristic show of restraint.

"Spit it out, Monica."

"Don't quit your dad." She finally looked up and I immediately wished she'd look away, but she wouldn't.

My cheeks heated and I felt dizzy. I leaned against a nearby stone wall.

"So you have a sister ..." Monica shrugged and sat next to me.

"Half sister," I corrected.

Georgia rolled her eyes and sat on the other side of me. "Fine. Half sister. There are worse things in life than having extra family." Her eyes fell along with her shoulders.

"Yeah," Monica continued, "Willow was the only person from your childhood I ever heard you mention with any frequency while we were in college. You said it was like you were sisters. Turns out you actually are."

I stood, facing my girlfriends. "I can't believe you two. My dad *lied* to me. And not about Santa Clause or the Tooth Fairy. Not only did he lie, but so did my mom and Willow's par—whatever."

Georgia stood, not looking one ounce sympathetic. "Right. And you still got to grow up with two loving parents who taught you it was okay, and, in fact, necessary to love hard and all the way to your core or whatever the fuck terminology your mom uses. You're allowed to feel railroaded, and to ask questions, and feel everything, but, please, don't you think given how you feel, your dad probably feels it more?"

I threw my head back in defiance. "How could he possibly?"

"Because he's been living with it for almost thirty years. Every single day. Letting Michael and Solstice raise Willow as their own. Jesus, I've only known your dad for like a minute compared to everyone else here, but that man is the most emotional brand of Y-chromosome I've come across. How many times do you think he wanted to pick up Willow and swing her around the way he did you? How many times do you think he watched Michael hold her while she cried and a piece of him didn't fall off of him and shrivel up in the dirt?" Georgia's chin quivered as she spewed her emotional assessment of my father.

One that was so accurate I had to sit again. I looked to Monica, who'd once again gone quiet, and I found tears in her eyes.

Her voice was soft. Cautious. "She's ... she's right, Ember."

Her confirmation pulled me under. Succumbing to the heavy honesty, I let the tears fall. "But they taught me about love ... everything I know."

Monica wrapped her arm around my shoulder. "And now they've taught you more. They loved you and Willow enough to give you each your own, unique, awesome families. Your mom loved your dad enough to stand by him when it would have been socially acceptable—if not expected—to leave. Your dad loved Michael enough to give him a daughter, and loved Willow enough as the years went on to leave her with the right family. *Her* family. And, he gave you yours."

Georgia shifted to my side. "You know ... my dad and I didn't have nearly the kind of relationship you and your dad do. Still, when he died, I felt like a lost toddler in the middle of a crowded beach. The ocean threatened to swallow me, people were pushing passed me, and even though I had my mom, I'd never felt so alone in my entire life."

"God," I put my head in my hands, "I've been so awful to him this week."

Monica kissed the top of my head. "And you know, because he loves you, that it doesn't matter to him. All that matters is you come home. To his heart. Wanna go do that?" She lifted my chin and gave me a hopeful smile.

A sob-soaked laugh crept from my throat as I stood and wiped under my eyes. My parents had raised me with nothing but love. That they'd engaged in a free-love lifestyle in their past was not a surprise to me. It was part of what led me to forge out a life of certainty for myself. Their choices—the ones I'd agreed and disagreed with—helped make me into the person I am.

My friends were right, though. The messy details and emotions could be sorted out later. The fact was, I was never—and would never—be in their shoes. Who was I to judge the decisions they made? Neither Willow nor I were ever lacking in attention or affection while growing up.

I wiped my tears once more. "Promise to hold my hand on the walk back?"

"Promise." Monica squeezed my hand.

I swear they sighed in unison. Georgia stood and spoke first, "Yes. Let's get you freshened up, though. You're all red and streaky from crying."

Monica held out her hand, and Georgia handed her a bag from a boutique we'd been in earlier.

"What's that?" I asked.

"I bought some make-up. You're going to use it." She winked at Georgia and started fussing with my face right there on the street.

"Guys," I laughed, "it's just my dad."

They stilled for a moment. Everything stilled.

"We know," Georgia said. "Just ... we know."

***

Twenty-five strange minutes later, Monica, Georgia, and I had finally returned to the campground. It was well past sunset, but the moon was bright enough to light our path back to the campsite.

"So, Mon, are you still going to stay for the Napa show?" I asked as we carefully navigated the root-covered ground.

"Yeah. Josh is coming out, too. He couldn't get a full two weeks off, so he'll join us ... now?" Monica's voice trailed off as Josh appeared in our path. "Josh?"

"Josh?" I echoed, my smile brightening.

Monica sped up and jumped when she reached him, and he squeezed her against his body. "You weren't supposed to be here yet!"

I couldn't hear him clearly through his whisper, but it sounded like he said, "Yes I was."

He set Monica down and walked to me. "Finnegan's misses you, Em." His boyish smile filled the space between us.

"Aw, I miss you, too. Josh." I gave him a tight hug, and turned to introduce him to Georgia.

"Josh, is it?" Georgia deadpanned as she stuck out her hand.

After all the reunions and introductions were out of the way, we finally made our way to the clearing of our campsite.

Where my dad was standing nervously, and alone, by a picnic table in the center of the site.

"Dad?" I looked behind me, only to find my friends silently retreating into the nearest RV.

Someone had taken electrical tape and spelled *The Mediator* on the side of the RV. I had no idea what that was about, but Monica and Regan seemed to be getting a laugh out of it.

Still confused, and feeling more nervous than I had in my whole life, I turned back to my dad, who was walking toward me, holding out his hand.

"Baby Blue," he whispered as our hands touched. He wasn't tentative in his embrace.

All anger and apprehension shot through the soles of my feet and spread across the earth around us as I cried heavy tears into his shoulder. Tears he, of course, returned onto mine.

It felt like every hug we'd ever shared, only this time there was something more.

"Dad," I sniffed as I pulled away, wiping my nose and under my eyes, "I'm sorry for being such a bitch ... I just ..."

He put up his hand, ignoring the desperate need to wipe his saturated cheeks. "I know. I know. I expected you to be angry, angel, I did. I expected a fight. But, when you just, shut down, I ... I thought I'd lost you." He grabbed my hand again and led me to the picnic table, sitting next to me on the long, cool rectangular bench.

"Well," I sighed, "as you know, it's not like this came totally out of the ... blue." I rolled my eyes and grinned to let the irony of the statement pass. He laughed softly. "Willow's been on my case about it for months."

My dad squeezed my hand, his clover-colored eyes drowning in uncertainty. "Why didn't you come to us right away?"

Why.

If there was ever any time to be honest, I'd learned over the last year, it was when you were surrounded with half-truths and lies. It was my chance to stand on my own two feet and own my feelings. Own my thoughts. Just. Own it.

"Because," I sighed as I rested my head on his shoulder, "I knew it was true. The second she said it, it was like my ears were flooded with the sound of a million *things* clicking into place ..." I trailed off as my tears dried.

My dad kissed the top of my head as he wrapped his arm around my back. "How'd you know?"

I shrugged. "I mean, the eyes, I guess, but that wasn't as solid for me as the other things. I always felt this strong connection with Willow. I knew how lucky I was to grow up with my best friend, and I often referred to her as "like a sister", but she always just *felt* like a sister. There was something ... just ... more there."

"What are you feeling now?"

"Well ... there were half a dozen times before we moved to Connecticut that Willow and I always said we wished we were *real* sisters so we could move together, and never have to live apart."

My dad cleared his throat. "Do you regret making that wish?"

With a deep sigh, I gave another honest answer. "No. It was confusing as hell, and still is a little bit. My knee jerk reaction was to conveniently toss everything you ever taught me about love out the window."

"Why didn't you?"

"Because if I hadn't learned from you, I wouldn't have Bo. I wouldn't have had the strength to let him go when he needed me to, or the strength to get back together when we were both ready. If it hadn't been for the kind of deep love you have, that all of you have, Willow and I wouldn't have had the lives we did." I sat up, looking him straight in the eyes. "I still have a lot of questions but ... you know what? I think our love is stronger than all of those questions and answers combined. Don't you?"

With a muffled cry, my dad pulled me back into a tear-filled hug. "It is, November. It absolutely is. And, when you're ready to ask, don't hesitate on a single one. I'll give you every answer I have."

It seemed like the more time I was spending with my family, the more solid ground I was given. Like going on this tour with them wasn't just an exercise in going back to my roots, but a process by which I was given a sturdy pair of wings.

And, at that exact moment, every single one of my dreams came true.

CHAPTER ELEVEN

...OLD, NEW, BORROWED, BLUE

Bo

As I watched Ember and her dad embrace on the picnic bench, Josh softly elbowed my side.

"Ready man?" he whispered.

I smiled, never moving my eyes from my future wife as she sat, unknowingly, only ten feet away. "I always have been."

The whole crew had sought refuge in the RV I'd been waiting in when Ember and her dad started talking. During the whole emotional ordeal my friends were more than quiet. Maybe watching me for signs of cold feet, all of them knowing what was going to happen next.

I turned to Georgia, who was nearest the power source. "Hit the lights, G."

With a grin that sent a twinkle to her eyes, Georgia moved to the end of the RV, and plugged in the extension cord.

I have to admit, I'd seen it once already, but the lights choked me up a bit. We used strings of white lights for many of our stage set-ups, so we always had totes full of them wherever we went. While Monica and Georgia distracted Ember all afternoon, Michael, Mags, and I strung as many lights as would fit between the trees surrounding the campsite, and crossways over them, creating a canopy of glowing white light.

As soon as the lights went on, Ember's back straightened. She looked startled as her head whipped from side to side. Her father, holding onto the last bit of composure I'm sure he had, sat back, took a deep breath, and watched her.

"Okay," I whispered to myself. "Let's go."

As I made my way down the aisle of the RV, Monica stopped me. The tears were already forming in her eyes.

"Thank you," she said as she wrapped her arms around my torso. "Thank you for being her soul mate."

"Thank you for letting me have her." I squeezed her back and gave her a smile as she pulled away.

"Nervous?" Regan questioned, stepping aside so I could get to the stairs.

I looked him up and down. "You got your violin ready?"

He nodded.

"Then, no. I'm not nervous. Excuse me, guys. That's my wife out there." As I pushed my hand against the door of the RV, I took one more breath.

Then, the realization of all of my dreams came rushing toward me.

"Bo?" Ember stood as she watched me exit the RV, eyeing me from head to toe.

While I wasn't in a tux, because that's not what we were about, I was in pressed khaki's and a black polo shirt. The nicest thing in my suitcase, and she knew it.

"Ember." I smiled and took her hands in mine, kissing her softly on the forehead. "I see things are okay with you and your dad?" I looked between them, certain I'd read the body language correctly, but needing confirmation if any of this was to go as planned.

Ember's chin quivered slightly as she smiled. "It is. We're okay."

I pulled her into a quick hug, savoring the scent of her hair for a second more.

"What is all of this?" she asked as she pulled away. "And where the hell is everyone?"

"We're right here," Raven answered as if this were all scripted. She exited the RV she'd been waiting in with the other band members.

"And here," Monica chirped as she led the rest of our friends down the stairs of the vehicle I'd been in.

Despite the soft, full glow of the lights surrounding us, I reveled in the sight of Ember's cheeks growing red as she tried to work out the scene. After looking at the happy—and somewhat weepy—faces of those around us, Ember whipped her head back around and looked at me, breathing heavily.

"Bo ..." Her lips curled up at the edges. A hopeful energy begging them to curl the rest of the way.

"November," I started, never breaking my gaze with hers, "what you and I have is something that I never knew was possible. Someone who loves everything inside me, including the things I didn't know were there. Or the things I didn't want to know were there. Someone who took each loss life handed to me and loved me through them, around them, and passed them. An actual mate to my bruised and battered soul."

Ember shook her head. "Not battered. Perfect."

I kissed her, our lips forming smiles against each other. "See?"

"What are you doing?" she whispered against my lips.

"Let me get to it," I answered, making her chuckle and sniff.

"Ember," I started again. "When I said it felt like I've loved you for a thousand lifetimes, I meant it. But, that's not enough for me." I placed my index finger under her chin and lifted her face. "I want one more."

I want one more was the only cue I'd given Regan. At that, he softly started playing a piece he and I had been working on for a couple of weeks. Ember's eyes filled with tears as they drifted to Regan and back to me.

A little over a year before, Ember walked in on me in my studio one of the first nights she stayed at my house in Concord. It was the middle of the night and I was having trouble sleeping, as usual. I'd gone into my studio to blow off some steam. Several minutes later, at Ember's innocent request that I play the sheet of music that was left on the piano, we were wrapped in the only song I'd ever written for that instrument. A song I'd written to encompass how I felt after my parents' death.

Regan and I transformed it. I wanted Ember to recognize it, and she did. I could tell by the way her hands tightened in mine and tears streaked down her cheeks. I wanted her, more than anything, to see how the song transformed from the darkness that was my life then, to the happiness it was now.

Because of her.

Ember and I had played a song in rehearsal a few times that we hadn't perfected for stage yet. I worked those measures into the middle of the song, and as Regan glided beautifully through them, Ember spoke.

"What did you do?" She smiled and cried at the same time. The absolute most beautiful sight in the world.

"I asked your father for his blessing in me asking you to marry me." I knew she meant the song. I answered the bigger question surrounding us.

"You ... you what?" Ember sniffed and looked at her father, who walked over to us and put an arm around her.

Ashby mirrored Ember's smile-cry. "This afternoon, angel, when you girls were downtown."

"But the lights," she gestured up, still smiling. "This was all done before ..."

"Love," I stepped back, placing my hands in my pocket, fishing for the ring box, "I knew things were rocky with you and your dad. I knew there are and were so many things to talk about. But, I knew you two *would* work it out, because I believe in love. And, I know you do, too. That's the only reason we made it this far."

Once my fingers were securely locked around the velvet box, I slowly lowered myself to one knee, trying to ignore the increase in sniffles from the group.

"I want you to marry me, Ember—"

Ember sank to both of her knees in front of me, her shoulders softly shaking as she cried. "Yes, Bo. I'll marry you."

We leaned toward each other, our foreheads meeting in the middle as our tears mixed.

"You didn't let me finish," I teased.

"There's more?" She laughed and cried as Regan's song finished and we were left in the silence of anticipation.

I opened the ring box.

"It was my mother's," I started, cutting her off preemptively. "Well, the stone was. I had it reset. For you. For us." My fingers felt like they'd tripled in size as I plucked the ring from its satin pillow.

I'd had the large diamond reset, nestled into a band of braided rose gold. Antique looking, and perfectly Ember.

"Your mother's," she whispered, her lips pursing together as she held out her hand. Her non-verbal commitment.

A slight sob escaped my mouth. "She would have loved you so much, Ember. They both would have. My sister was crazy about you ..." I took a deep breath. Rather than let sorrow drown me, I let the spirits of my departed family members lift me up and hold me against the woman that I loved.

Despite being in the dirt, and surrounded by family and friends, Ember and I stayed in our private moment for a few seconds longer, breathing in the serenity we brought to each other.

Finally, Ember spoke. "Can I say yes yet?"

I slid the ring on her slender finger, watching my mother's diamond catch the light from the tiny strands of lights hanging over us. "Almost."

"There's more?" She sniffed and leaned back as the ring settled into perfect placement.

"I want to do it now."

Ember's eyebrows pulled together. "You've asked me."

"I want to marry you now. Tonight. Here. There's nothing we could plan that could possibly be more perfect than this moment. Right here. Me. You. Our family and friends. I've wanted to marry you since the very second I met you, Ember. I don't want to wait any more."

Ember slowly rose to standing, tugging my hands so I'd follow. The humidity ran her waves in wild patterns around her face and shoulders. Her tears seemed to dry in an instant, and I was shaking as I waited for her response. Though the fire in her yes gave me all the answer I needed.

After an eternity and a half, her shoulders rose as she took a deep breath, and sank again as she exhaled. "Right now." She smiled and bit her lip. "I want to be your wife tonight. And tomorrow morning, and for all the mornings we have left. And, even after those run out. I'll marry you tonight, Bo Cavanaugh, because I've been waiting for you to ask since before I even knew you."

The world got loud, then. The sound of our bodies crashing into an incredible kiss. One we usually saved for the privacy rarely afforded to us. Squeals from her friends and parents and band members, and slaps on the back from Regan and Josh were like the champagne bottle breaking on a newly christened ship.

"Wait," Ember shook her head, seeming to try to shake some sense into herself, "how? How can we, tonight?"

I looked through the small crowd and locked eyes with Journey, who graciously placed her hand on Ember's shoulder.

"If you'll have me," Journey stated kindly, "I'd love to officiate. Of course you'll need to handle the license and all of that in the morning ... but, hell, that's just paperwork. We can join you tonight. If you'd like."

Ember looked at me hopefully. "Are you okay with that?"

I grinned. "I already asked her."

"I can't wear this." Ember seemed to start to panic, but her mom, Monica, and Georgia fluttered to her side in an instant.

"I've got a dress for you, sweetie." Raven wrapped her arms around her daughter and me at the same time. "I'm just beside myself for you two."

"Wait!" Ember shouted, striking silence through the crowd. "Daddy?"

On command, Ashby moved next to his daughter. "What is it?"

"You said it was okay, right?"

Everyone broke into loud laughter as Ember and her dad hugged again. It was a beautiful sight, given the past few days.

"He's a good man, Ember. And, if I have to let you go," his voice pinched as he wiped under his eyes, "it could be to no one better."

Ember pulled her dad closer. "You're not letting me go," I caught her whisper into his ear.

"Okay," Ember said as she pulled away from her dad. "I need to freshen up."

Georgia and Monica stepped forward. Before they could say anything, a small rental sedan screeched it's way to the campsite, stopping just behind the RV.

The door flew open in a flash, and Willow ejected from the driver's seat, running toward us. "Did I miss it? Did I miss it? I got here as fast as I could!" She caught up with Ember, panting with her hands on her hips.

Suddenly everyone's eyes were on me once again. I shrugged. "Everyone needed to be here." I held my breath that I'd made the right choice in calling Willow during her road trip back to San Diego.

Apparently everyone else was holding their breath, too, because the air seemed really quiet as Ember and Willow stared at each other.

"I'm so happy you're here," Ember wept as she drew Willow into a hug.

Willow squeezed her arms around Ember even tighter. "Are you kidding? This is all we talked about when we were little. I'd never miss it."

Through the mixture of sighs and tears, Georgia and Monica commanded attention once again.

"I'm cupcakes and hair." Georgia smiled and put her hands on her hips.

"And I'm jewels and makeup. Let's go." Monica grabbed Ember's hand and led her into the RV I'd waited in for what seemed like hours this afternoon.

While everyone bustled around me, placing freshly-picked wildflowers at the table and talking about who was going to sit where, I kept my feet rooted in the spot she'd said *yes*, and the spot where we'd soon—sort of officially—become husband and wife.

My favorite spot in the entire universe.

***

Less than ten minutes later, the door to the RV cracked, and Ashby grinned as he held it in place. I was so lost in the exchange, I didn't notice Raven sneak up beside me.

"Let's have a look at you," Raven cooed as she turned me toward her. "That was a nice thing you did. With Willow and Ember …"

"It was nothing, Raven. It seemed like the right thing to do." I never in a million years before this morning thought I'd ever call Willow Shaw for anything. Turns out, for my future wife, I'd do exactly anything.

Her hands smoothed over my shoulders and brushed across the front of my shirt before she dropped her hands to my wrists and held them tightly.

"They're here, you know." She brought our hands to my chest over my heart. "They're always here."

I lowered my head for a moment, the one intimate moment I hadn't planned on happening tonight. One between me and Raven. And my deceased family. My jaw clenched briefly and I let my eyes fill with tears.

"I miss them," I admitted, holding her hand tighter.

Raven's long reddish hair had grey streaks weaving through its waves, leaving me smiling as I thought about how Ember and I might look when our children married. "I know you do, honey." Raven smiled and wriggled one of her hands free to place under my chin. "And no one can, or could try, to replace them. But we'll keep loving the hell out of you. You've given Ashby and me the greatest gift anyone could have given us. You helped our daughter believe everything we ever taught her. You made it real to her. You make her happy and keep her safe. You're absolutely everything we could have ever asked for."

Before I could answer, Regan struck the bow across the strings of his violin, signaling Ember's approach. Pachelbel's Canon in D Major sent goosebumps across my back. I'd heard the song played at a million weddings before, and never felt that reaction. Tonight, however, was different. Tonight it signaled that *my* wife was on her way.

"Here she comes." I tilted my head toward the end of our makeshift aisle, lined with daisy petals.

"You'll do perfect," Raven whispered. She gave my cheek a quick kiss, then scurried a few feet in front of me to stand and wait for Ember and Ashby.

Georgia and Monica were the first out of the RV, holding tiny bunches of wildflowers. They'd changed into casual summer dresses, and walked with wide smiles toward me, stopping next to Raven.

Monica wiped under her eyes several times, and I heard her cursing her mascara under her breath.

All of that faded into the periphery as I watched Ember's hand reach for her dad's and he led her down the stairs of the RV. The hem of the long, white, strapless dress her mother altered for her from her own collection of clothes brushed against the ground as she walked toward me.

While she clutched her father's hand tightly, and he watched her with soft admiration as they walked, her eyes never left mine. No longer glistening with tears, her eyes were just like the first night I met her. Fierce. Glowing.

Her hair was half up, pinned on the side with a sparkly clip that had what looked like diamonds and emeralds in it. I'd seen Raven hand it to Monica before they boarded the RV, and it highlighted the depth of her eyes the closer she got to me.

Realistically speaking, the walk from the RV to me was only about twenty feet, but the wait was excruciating. When Ashby and Ember finally reached me, Ashby embraced his daughter once more, holding her at arms length before turning to me.

He put her hand in mine and squeezed our hands together, eyeing me.

"Take care of her," was all he said before sniffling and taking his place next to Raven.

"You're stunning," I said as I pulled her close to me, kissing her softly on the cheek. We'd ignored every other conventional wedding protocol, why stop now?

Ember swallowed hard, and I could tell she was trying to ward off tears. "Thank you. For tonight, and forever."

Journey had been standing just to my side the entire time, but only spoke once Ember and I were joined, and turned to face her. Her smile was as wide as Embers, and as wide as mine felt.

"Ready?" she asked, moving her eyes between us.

In unison, Ember and I looked over our shoulders, into the loving eyes of those standing behind us. Standing for us. We looked back into each others eyes and answered Journey.

"We are."

And, that is the story of how I married Ember. Under the glow of twinkle lights somewhere in Northern California, we pledged for better or worse, for richer or pooler, and in sickness and health.

Boy, did we do that in the nick of time.

$T_2\ H_2\ E_1\quad E_1\ N_1\ D_1$

Made in the USA
Monee, IL
01 April 2024